UNTITLED *Life's* RANDOM LESSONS

A tapestry of anecdotes on life, mindset, leadership, communication and relationships

Ramesh Sood

INDIA • SINGAPORE • MALAYSIA

ISBN 979-8-89133-996-5

Dedicated

To Life and The Best In You!

LEGAL DISCLAIMER

A NOTE BEFORE WE BEGIN

Dear Reader,

I thought it was better to write it short and relevant. Not everyone has the time and patience to read full length books for some serious learning. Hope you will find this book useful having picked it up; and that you will find a friend in it whenever the need arises.

It's random, free from any boundaries or titles, every page is independent. Just open it in any place and see, feel or hear from your heart. Has life led you to that page? It's just like when one picks up some grains in one's fist and scatters them around and then picks them up randomly and keeps them together. This is a collection of my daily posts on LinkedIn.

The stories & anecdotes are based on my own and others' real-life experiences. It is possible that my intense reading habit of almost five decades influenced my thoughts and writing over the years. I acknowledge all the great writers from whom I have learned.

Life is all about learning & sharing.

With best wishes!

Ramesh Sood

***#simplySOOD**(TM)*

November 10, 2023

UNTITLED #1

I remember sitting at a friend's place and noticing his little children playing together, their hands full of chocolates gifted by me.

Suddenly the elder one pulled the younger one's hand that held the chocolates.

All the chocolates fell on the floor.

He immediately picked up two chocolates for himself. The younger one cried. He wanted them back. Elder one refused to give it back.

That's when the younger one threw the rest of the chocolates too and shouted, "I don't want any. I don't care. Keep all of them," and angrily stomped out of the house.

The elder was happy to keep all the chocolates. My friend appeared quite aloof and sheepishly told me, "They are like that. Don't bother."

I am afraid the younger one would face and react the same way in similar situations when he grows up unless some corrective action is taken by my friend now.

Be it any stage in life, never decide to leave behind what's yours just because of some emotional outburst. Stay cool.

Protect what belongs to you and then work diligently to regain what was taken away, if ever.

Mind you, I am also talking about the credit which often gets smartly stolen in the workplace by manipulative minds.

UNTITLED #2

"Hey, you are extraordinary."

I addressed my colleague (also a good friend)

He folded his hands and made an earnest request, almost whispering in my ears,

"Please don't repeat these words".

"Why?" I wanted to know.

"I am scared. Never speak like that openly. I may become a target for many ordinary souls. They may join hands and make me an EXTRA."

What do you think must have happened?

The moment you get identified by someone as extraordinary and people start talking about you in awe, at that very moment, an opposite action starts:

In some hearts, a desire to pull you down takes birth.

It can be more intense than yours. So, be cautious.

Life taught me one thing for sure. You need not be extraordinary. Yet, don't remain ordinary. Instead, be a little more than ordinary, and let it be very subtle. It takes a lifetime of making mistakes to learn the magic of right living. Yet, it is very interesting and satisfying.

UNTITLED #3

I reached Bangalore Airport to catch my return flight to Pune over a weekend.

Oh, it was a complete mess, a terrible rush & total chaos. I was an integral part of the chaos too.

Yet, I knew which flight I had to catch.

Everyone, just like me, moved towards their destinations in just the right way, as if it was a perfect design.

This made me think about life. If I ever face chaos, I should remember that it won't last forever. A hidden perfect design will guide me to my destination. All I need to do is be patient, take small steps, and stay alert to overcome the chaos at the right time.

I shall ensure that I don't get stuck.

One tiny step is all you might need sometimes.

Exactly like I did in that long queue, moving at a snail's pace till I reached the area where I could make some big strides.

UNTITLED #4

Do you have someone who tries to stop you from doing things by instilling fear? Maybe it's a well-wisher, a close associate, a colleague, or a friend.

Haven't you met people who control you through your own fears, sometimes for years, without you even realising it?

They try to prevent you from experiencing the joy of exploring new possibilities because they don't want you to face any harm.

In a corporate setting, haven't many of us either killed our own ideas or allowed others to shut them down because we were afraid of problems?

I found a way to counter this.

Now, whenever someone warns me or tries to discourage me from pursuing an idea by generating fear, I always ask one simple question.

"How do you know it?"

And that has made all the difference.

UNTITLED #5

When I was studying in 8th grade, We had just shifted to a bigger house from a smaller one. I had to change my school as well. In fact, A better school. I made many new friends.

One of them, who I thought could be my best friend, invited me to his house to play.

Meanwhile, My family decided to go to a movie and insisted I join them.

But I was excited to meet my friend. I denied them.

When I reached his home. My friend was standing outside his house along with his sister.

Suddenly a car came out of the gate, being driven by his father with his mother sitting beside home, my friend saw me and shouted from a distance,

"Sorry, but I am going to watch a movie with my family."

I stood there like a statue.

Life had given me a subtle lesson there. I was too young to pick it up. And it took me many more years before I understood and learned.

Today I am convinced about this one thing. One can never practice 100 per cent happiness without living by this one principle, one credo: ***Family First.***

UNTITLED #6

He was a man of almost my age. We were travelling in Shatabdi from New Delhi to Ludhiana. (4-hour journey)

He had been talking to the person sitting on the other side, and from his talk, he appeared to be a businessman. All his talk sounded from a place of arrogance about being rich.

He asked me, "What do you do?" when I was pulling my bags out from the loft.

I looked at him and wondered about the timing of his asking me the question.

"I am a Mindset & Behavior Trainer," I replied.

"What is that?" He asked me.

"Well, I help people become self-aware by getting them to understand their thinking patterns. Then if they want, I work with them and help them change themselves. "

He frowned, made a face and threw his arms in the air, almost exclaiming with great force.

"What!? No one can change another person. Such a person doesn't exist."

What a sweeping statement that was!

I thought of responding to him. But he wasn't in a frame of mind to listen to a different view than his. So I didn't.

UNTITLED #7

When I look back, I find it so funny.

Until recently, the assumed reasons for others' success and my failures were the same.

LUCK. Ha, ha!

Now I know that it was TRUE.

The only added learning is that they attracted 'Good Luck' because of their efforts, and I attracted 'Bad Luck' because of my behaviour.

Learning this one truth helped me.

It might help you as well.

UNTITLED #8

This is the story of the best compliment I ever received.

The Chairman, MD and some of his VIP guests from abroad were having a plant tour on one of the season's hottest days.

It was decided that during this visit, they would stop at a designated place where they would be served some refreshments.

We made all the arrangements by placing an attendant. The guests were supposed to arrive at 1200 hrs. At about 1145 hrs, the attendant asked for a few minutes to the washroom. He promised to return in about 07-08 minutes as he had to walk some distance. Since there was some time left, I agreed and let him go.

Behold! The moment he left, the caravan of cars arrived, and VIPs alighted.

Who would offer them the water?

I spontaneously decided to serve and carried the tray of water.

As I reached our MD, he picked up his glass with his right hand & put his left hand under the tray to squeeze my right one and released while lightly patting it.

Even in moments like those, He found a way to give compliments and appreciation. I will always remember this beautiful gesture.

UNTITLED #9

The other day, I was buying vegetables and fruits from the corner shop near my house.

While packing, the boy at the sales counter put tomatoes and grapes first. He topped them with harder items like cauliflower, apples and watermelon etc., in the same bag.

Simple common sense would have made him keep softer items on the top.

I objected to the way it was packed and demanded two separate bags.

He made a bad face, repacked the items and pushed the packet towards me. Well, those were my vegetables & fruits, which were to get cut or cooked & served with all the care and love. I refused to pick up the packet and told him politely that he would have to hand over the packet to me with a smile. I just stood there, looking at him, smiling.

Finally, mirror neurons worked. He couldn't avoid the effect and smiled and then laughed. Oh, he had to because I have made a rule not to let anyone transact with me in a bad mood. I don't permit it.

Either I postpone the interaction or I make the person change his state. ***And when it comes to selling, well, people must smile to sell!***

UNTITLED #10

As the discussion turned intense,

He suddenly revealed what could be considered something very personal.

I felt a bit surprised and asked, "Why should you share this?"

He was very candid & clear,

"Sir, I feel unburdened."

I was uncomfortable and said, "But how can you trust me?"

He replied, "Sir, I choose to trust you,"

I wanted to still make him aware, "If I betray you, then?"

He looked at me with great intensity and said, "That will be your choice".

In those moments, I realised that you can never get a bigger compliment than someone saying, "I trust you." I learned to choose trust. We can choose to become trustworthy to let life smile more.

UNTITLED #11

"Sir, I am so very irritated with this person. I can't tolerate his voice & the tone with which he talks to his team. I hate him", she was really angry.

"Are you in his team?" I asked.

"No, sir, but we sit near to each other. He doesn't dare talk like that to me."

"So, what is the issue?" I asked.

"Sir, it's bad, you know. I keep thinking: *Why is he like that?*"

I advised, "Just remove the *"Why"* and speak the rest of the sentence loudly".

She shouted, "He is like that!" Her expressions first contorted, then appeared confused, and finally eased.

I asked her to say it once more. She was pretty loud, "He is like that!"

"Yes, he is like that. Now decide how you want to handle him." She understood & smiled. Removing one word from self-talk suddenly transformed her.

UNTITLED #12

It was his farewell party.

He was my mentor, one of the most sophisticated, polished and well-mannered senior executives.

I was a bit sad when he found me standing alone.

He walked towards me from his group and patted me on my shoulder. I was overwhelmed.

Greeting him, I said, "Sir, this being your last day, would you like to give me one piece of advice that will hold me in good stead?"

He contemplated my question and said, "Remember, in a corporate, you can either become popular by keeping everyone pleased or perform to the best of your potential to help the organisation grow. Your choice will define you."

I chose the latter and happily struggled.

UNTITLED #13

On my way to a supermarket near our house, I met an acquaintance and casually asked, “Hi, where are you going?”

He looked at me, smiled and politely asked, “Why?”

I was stunned.

I didn’t have a reason and couldn’t make one.

I just gave him a smile and moved on.

After thinking over it, I realised it was one of the most powerful responses to personal questions people tend to ask.

I have since used it well and perhaps avoided many unnecessary conversations.

UNTITLED #14

Is it true that we like those people more who make us like ourselves?

We like that part of the person which is more like us.

We know that just a step outside us is a magical beginning to a life so vast & beautiful.

Taking that one step is the most difficult part of a journey that each one of us wants to undertake, but we generally don't.

Our fears hold us.

Overcoming those fears and falling in love with ourselves for the first time could be such a beautiful experience because only then will we be able to accept and like other people for what they are.

UNTITLED #15

"Why can't you understand what I am telling you? I don't know how many times I have to tell."

I shouted at a Trainee.

We were informally meeting in the lounge of our club.

A senior guest incidentally sitting nearer heard me.

After the trainee left, he asked me if he could share something. I consented, and he said,

"Never shout at people like that. It's not about what and how you say it. It's more about how they understand it. What is their mode of understanding?

If they fail to understand you, it doesn't make them unintelligent or people with low IQ.

But yes, it makes you someone who doesn't understand people. You need to learn."

I learnt..

UNTITLED #16

The other day as I drove on the road, I felt the car ahead of me was going too slow. I found it so stupid because I had to find space and over-take it from the wrong side.

And then another car just sped by, overtaking me in a hush. It went very fast. I cursed – Mad fellow!

What was happening in my mind? You go slower than me, then you are stupid; you go faster, then you are mad. And there is no space for driving by my side. Yes, think about it.

We want people to walk with us, but we don't leave any space. So, perhaps, we must learn & create that space however little we can. Even in our business meetings with our teams, we need to do it and let them walk along with us. What say?

UNTITLED #17

People ask how I handle negative emotions to practice happiness. My answer still is

Envy: Wow, they are better than me. Let me work on myself.

Jealous: Lucky me. I never feel jealous. Some people tell me that my head injuries in childhood must have affected the area responsible for jealousy.

No, you need not take the same route. It is simple - Tell yourself that someone better ahead awaits you. And keep moving forward.

Anger: I watch it arise and then let it go instantly. Yes, on some rare occasions, it disturbs the positive energy around but then I can regenerate quickly.

Hurt: Oh, no, I don't ever give that consent to anyone.

Guilt: Past doesn't stay. Seek forgiveness. Forgive yourself and learn.

Regret: Why?

UNTITLED #18

I completed 35 years of my professional life on March 05, 2017. A new associate asked me to share what one thing, the most profound, I learned in all those years. Well, here it is:

When someone is talking good to you doesn't mean they are also thinking good of you; it doesn't mean they are feeling good about you. In fact, people tend to be sweeter with you when they have been talking bad behind your back. So, be careful always.

UNTITLED #19

"I am special & unique, just like you too are," he said. And this understanding made him a little better than me.

UNTITLED #20

HR Manager was happy. It was his turn to grill the candidate.

Because he was an athlete, a book lover, watched movies, enjoyed serials, and kept himself updated with news, he could always catch people on the wrong foot. He looked into the eyes of the candidate and asked,

"Tell me about your hobby."

The candidate gave him a confident smile and said, "Gardening."

And well, HR Manager looked at him and said, "Hmm, that's a good hobby. A nice hobby."

UNTITLED #21

Have you noticed that for a mistake of the subordinate, you get angry and even shout?

However, when your boss makes a mistake, you neither shout nor get angry. Instead, you help your boss not to get upset and willingly own that mistake.

It proves only one thing - If we want, we can consciously control our emotions, even anger. Yes, we can. We are the masters. And not slaves to our emotions. Yes, think about it.

UNTITLED #22

We tend to develop dislike for those in whose presence we are not able to like ourselves.

Remember better to feel inspired and respect such people because they can help us evolve to a higher state.

UNTITLED #23

Ancient wisdom says that those who can conceal themselves live well. And it holds so true today also. We keep on talking in admiration of those who talk less, who hardly ever talk about themselves.

UNTITLED #24

He cleaned the dust; the book looked at him, shedding invisible tears, almost cried and pleaded,

"Hey, will you open me, at least now that I finally see you around? Let the words tied up in my pages speak out for once. I am bound to hold them together, but then I won't mind if you let them spill and share with others. Isn't that why you picked me up in the first place? Please let me be used for the purpose I exist. Let me get read." He didn't answer.

Books looked so beautiful lined up in an array of colourful strips. Friends visiting him always felt in awe of him for his collection and perceived him to be an intellectual.

UNTITLED #25

I was playing against a senior player. It was a Pre-quarter final of the State TT Championships. The year was 1979.

5th game

I made it a deuce 20-20 from 16-19, then the score became 28-29. I served, and the man hit a topspin, and the ball just nudged the edge of the table, and lo, behold, I stood there. I had lost.

And when I look back at this match, it reminds me of a few more where luck had played its role which often became a decisive factor.

Simply Means - time plays a trick. I learned that we should take it all in stride with humility. We should keep playing in the space beyond winning and losing.

UNTITLED #26

"My boss doesn't listen to me."

The most common complaint ever.

Solution is simple - Is there someone whom you don't listen to? Check what they are doing to you which makes you resist listening to them.

Can you do the same with your boss?

You may resolve a big issue.

UNTITLED #27

I saw him running with his office bag dangling from his shoulder. He had to catch the cab.

An acquaintance said it was an everyday story. I was surprised. It was so easy to rewrite this story.

One had to go back and look at each sentence and change some commas or semicolons or use some easier, shorter words. Will he ever understand or realise this?

UNTITLED #28

He told me he was a leadership coach.

I asked him, "How long have you led people or teams before becoming a coach?"

A young man, about 29. He gave me a real mocking look and said, "Why? I have an international certification. I have paid through my nose to become one. I am trained. I can coach. Why did you ask me a question like that? "

Indeed, who was I to ask such a question? He had just introduced himself... I apologised, and we changed the subject.

UNTITLED #29

Sometime in 2018, I was called for a meeting, and after talking about the desired outcome, the young HR executive said,

"Sir, I am sure you will be conducting a lot of games during the one-day session."

I wondered and asked,

"Why you want to have so many games?"

He replied, "Sir, games keep people active. They participate well."

I asked, "If they can stay focused through intense interaction, then why are games necessary?"

He appeared restless and said, "But they expect that. You know otherwise, people tend to get bored." I smiled and took his leave. Do I have to share the result?

UNTITLED #30

"Sir, I have an idea. I want to give," the Passionate Young Employee (PYE) said.

"Have I asked you?" Sir was rude.

"Here it is, sir. I am giving it," and the PYE offers the idea.

Sir glares and snubs him, "Why are you trying to spend energies where you shouldn't."

"I thought it was part of my job to give ideas for improvement. I have given it to help ease your work and reduce costs. You don't want it. You have a dustbin." PYE got emotional and left.

After three months, His boss was facilitated for the same idea by the MD of the company. I know you are NOT a boss like that.

UNTITLED #31

Boss: "How are you?"

Employee: "Fine, sir!"

Boss: "Well, you won't be fine in the next two minutes..."

Then the boss criticised him for the mistake boss had made.

Manager: "How are you?"

Employee: "Fine, sir!"

Manager: "I gave you the wrong instruction. You followed it blindly. Now correct it."

He: "Sorry, sir."

Manager: "Hmm."

Leader: "How are you?". He: "Fine, sir!".

Leader: "Well, I made an error today and gave you the wrong instructions. Sorry for that".

He: "Please, sir, it's my fault too. I should have been careful. I will correct it."

Leader: OK, now do like this...

And you know what is funny about this. One can be all three depending upon one's like or dislike for the person one is talking to. Think about it.

UNTITLED #32

The biggest danger of walking alone on the right path is that many will interrupt to tell you that you are walking on the wrong path. And they would be the same people who appreciated you and praised you on your earlier path, which you realised was wrong for you. Stay strong and keep walking.

UNTITLED #33

We are talking about exponential technological change and feel concerned about whether we can keep up with the pace of change. I am concerned about another change.

One day as I drove, a 20-year-old almost brought his speeding bike on me and then glared at me with an angry and distorted expression. Mind you, I was driving on my side.

Yes, I am concerned about this explosive change in behaviour. Are you too?

UNTITLED #34

I remember writing letters and then waiting patiently, sometimes for a month or more, to get a response. Today, if the WhatsApp message sent doesn't show that pair of ticks changing colour in as little a time as an hour (or a few minutes?). We feel sad, we feel neglected, which upsets us. We can't wait anymore. We need everything in an instant.

We have lost that trait, that most crucial trait, patience. We need to bring it back. We need to practice it. Wisdom includes patience. Let us once again become wiser.

UNTITLED #35

A 5-year-old walked into the TT room. I was about to collide with her while playing a shot. I asked her to sit. She paused, looked at me & my partner and said, "Sorry, uncle, I was watching you from up there. I came down to tell you both that you play very well."

There was a 5-year-old taking time to appreciate us because she liked watching our game. Amazing!

Of course, she hadn't undergone any training. That day I got convinced that leaders are born. Either one has it or hasn't. If one has it, then better to spot and hone and polish skills and talent and make him/her emerge.

UNTITLED #36

May 16, 2017.

As we slowly settle into our newly rented apartment, I look back at the hectic, stressful, irritating moments when we got busy unpacking and settling our older furniture in a new space. And well, it's so natural. Unpacking and rearranging is always difficult, particularly when one can't copy the earlier arrangement in the new environment and space.

Isn't it the same with our minds and our beliefs? Rearrangement is so very difficult and frustrating.

And you know what I finally learned. Once you pass through those tough moments. You find it all so beautiful.

As I find the change from a permanent view of some or the other person smoking on the balcony of an office complex to a panoramic view of the city as nights make it sparkle.

Yes, change is difficult, yet it turns out to be beautiful despite those hectic, stressful, irritating moments of transition.

UNTITLED #37

He asked, "How can you practice happiness all the time?"

"Because I can," I answered.

"What can really make you feel happy in this moment?" he appeared adamant to prove me wrong.

It was time to ask a question. So, I asked him with a smile, "Why would I not be happy meeting you and talking to you? Tell me? Should I feel unhappy?"

He looked at me and said with a bit of sadness in his voice, "Didn't know I could be such a person? "

I wondered about his own opinion of him. "Well, now you know. There are some people around who do like us and feel happier in our presence. We need to spend time with them. That's the choice we need to make,"

I told him, and I'm telling you too. Aren't you too such a person in whose presence some people do feel happy? You know that you are. So be!!

UNTITLED #38

Some experiences in the last few days have taught me something very profound. We can say whatever we want with however good intentions or a pious meaning. Yet, everything depends on how the receivers receive it. Haven't I seen some relationships losing their sheen only because whatever gets communicated is taken with the opposite meaning?

I learned that what I say is not important. What you hear and what meaning you give to what I say is more important. So the best I can do to save a relationship or keep the gates of communication open is to take responsibility for a failed communication if it is initiated by me. It means I must ensure that my communication reaches you carrying the same meaning it is intended to give. If you are listening to something that I actually don't mean, then I have failed in my communication.

Hope I am able to reach you, the reader, as clearly as I can. Let me know.

UNTITLED #39

Coolie (Porter) had left our luggage and gone for a stroll, as there was some more time to go before our train arrived. Well, those few moments passed by, and I saw the train arriving. I looked around for our coolie (porter) and spotted him coming towards us at some distance.

I stayed focused on him when I saw him pulling a small child who had bent forward, standing on the edge of the platform and making him stand at a safe distance without anyone around noticing it. Elders with the child appeared busy on mobiles. When I appreciated our coolie (Porter), he just smiled.

It was yet another reminder that we needed to carefully & critically look at our use of mobiles. We will have to ensure that those are kept in our pockets in situations which demand our attention and concentration on more important and valuable things/tasks than responding to or looking at regular WhatsApp feed. Someone may say that those adults could be busy reading some important messages. Well, what can be more important than the safety of the child? What do you say?

UNTITLED #40

He was happy. Despite his doubts, his boss had brought him along when he expressed his desire to attend the event. He could see the owner's family there at the facility's gate, having arrived before them.

He will have an opportunity to say hello and introduce himself to them. After almost two decades of hard work, he deserved it as he was known just as a name often published in the house journal. They were pretty near when his boss turned towards him and said, "Hey, I think I have left my car door open. Go and close it."

He had to turn and return to the car where a watchman stood. The car didn't need to be locked. It was in a private area with the security head to report to the boss. Still, he locked it, turned to look at the gate and found that there was none. And suddenly, he heard the sound of clapping, a huge applause.

Ribbon had been cut. He understood and walked back quietly to his office. As he walked, he decided what he would never do in his life and then wrote to remember and live it forever: "Oh, God, help me live with just this one credo. If I can't give light to someone, let me hold none in my shadow."

UNTITLED #41

One thing that keeps me going distances is what I have experienced every time. It doesn't matter how far I go. I have always been able to return home.

UNTITLED #42

Teachers taught me how to write the alphabet. My mom made me practice it at home. When I look back, I realise that school didn't have that much time to help me with sufficient practice of what I learned, and therefore, I would be asked to do some homework which meant practising inputs with the help of my mom.

After growing up, I attended training, many a time, like a class in school, where I was given inputs and occasionally a little initial practice. Alas, I didn't have anyone to help me with that practice at home because now I was grown up. None compelled me like my mom or my dad, or my elder sister did earlier. Finding time to practice was my responsibility. My lack of will to do that ultimately made the training ineffective. I needed only one thing to learn, and that was self-motivation.

Nothing else.

Well, I couldn't buy an injection of motivation from any medicine shop. Yet, I needed to inject myself with motivation. It was no more available outside. It had to come from inside. I took a dive into my inner depths and picked up my gleaming dreams, and don't be surprised, my fears too.

Yes, these two combined to make me self-motivated- One, fear of survival in a changing world; Two, the hope of fulfilment of dreams in a world of possibilities. Is there any other way? Tell me.

UNTITLED #43

Standing on the edge of a mountain road, I was awestruck by the splash of colours in the valley spread in front of me as a splendid sun dipped slowly. I couldn't hold myself and shouted -I WANT TO BE HAPPY LIKE THIS ALWAYS -and from that moment onward, I started finding ways to be happy.

Yes, I consciously practice happiness. Trust me, it is possible.

No, it's not that I don't find negative emotions arising occasionally; I can understand them, accept them and reciprocate by slowly melting them away.

No, they don't stay to add to my moments of discomfort. You know, sometimes happiness just arrives, like, the other day, a butterfly sat on my left shoulder. Happiness had come flying. I let the butterfly go, and happiness stayed.

UNTITLED #44

The world is indeed changing very fast. I had the firsthand experience of it sometime in 2018. I was on a personal/professional visit to Ludhiana and some other cities in Punjab. I didn't carry my mobile charger along as I thought it would be available in the cars I was going to travel for my visit to a couple of clients.

It was available but only for iPhones and not for my Samsung Galaxy series mobile.

Was I already getting outdated, having just started communicating with a Smart Phone? Your guess is as good as mine. I learned that I will have to change my speed to adapt in many other areas. This is just one example. I am ready.

Are you?

UNTITLED #45

While life initiated this lesson some 30 years ago, it took me many years to learn. We can never know when and where, and in what disguise we will meet our match who would outsmart us.

It happened three decades ago. I hired a pedal rickshaw from Chaura Bazar, Ludhiana, to Kailash Cinema on one of my visits to my home town after I had settled in Maharashtra.

I was being charged by the rickshaw puller a lot more than what would be the normal case. As the rickshaw entered a a long stretch with a slope I told the rickshaw puller, "Hey, you don't even have to pedal it for such a long distance. It is so easy. You have charged me more.

He heard me and asked, "Do you really think it is easy?: I was more than clear, so I responded assertively, "Yes, it is easy. There is no effort.".

He stopped, got down and told me straight on my face, "Sahib (Sir), let us exchange seats, then we will see."

UNTITLED #46

"I play with him and control him using strategies, my bright-eyed and ambitious subordinate there," he boasted, looking at the young guy sitting on a sofa in the club lobby turning magazine pages.

"Oh, is it? To play with him, you must be doing certain things," the wise one asked.

"Of course, I must plan, plot and execute," he said.

"To do those things, you spend time; for me, time is life."

"What?" he appeared confused.

"If there is no life, there is no time. You have time because you are living. Dead don't have time. So any time spent is a life spent".

"What exactly do you want to say?"

"Simple. You spend a portion of your life working on strategies to control his life because of what he is," the wise one couldn't have made it simpler.

He didn't speak.

The wise one ended the conversation by saying, "So actually, he controls your life by being what he is. It is not the other way around. You may think like that. But the truth is that he controls you without your awareness."

UNTITLED #47

As I woke up today morning, I suddenly found an incident from the past appearing in my thoughts.

About two decades ago, one day, as I was almost jogging, not walking, on the long stretch of road, I came face to face with that old man who had a shining glow on his face and a very peaceful expression. The man had looked at me, smiled and gave me a thumbs-up. Oh, I had felt happy as for me, it was indeed a super compliment. That simple gesture filled me with lots of positive energy.

As I remembered it, I found myself getting re-energised. Good for the day, I felt. With the incident live in my mind, feeling lighter, I went out for my regular walk after my prayers which included saying a happy hello to the rising sun. After I had covered some distance, I saw two youngsters jogging and coming towards me. Somehow, they appeared attracted, maybe due to my shining grey hair and threw a glance at me. I spontaneously gave them a thumbs-up with a smile. OMG, their faces suddenly got lit up, eyes sparkled, and they smiled back, wishing me a highly energised "Good Morning, sir" together in one voice as they went past me. I was filled with a feeling of great delight as I suddenly found more springs in my feet.

UNTITLED #48

My life changed absolutely some years ago when I read this old Zen saying and deeply contemplated upon it: "Zen is just picking up your coat from the floor and hanging it up."

Simple. I just started 'doing' all that was needed. I have always spotted a 'coat' lying, and I have done all that is needed to be done to pick it up with or without support. Nothing wrong in seeking support when we need it.

UNTITLED #49

I was late and therefore rushed fast on my 'Scooty', which suddenly jumped and almost fell. A voice called out, "Thanks a lot!! "I looked around, and there was none.

The voice continued, "Don't look around. I am the speed-breaker talking to you."OMG, I was perplexed and didn't know how to respond.

So I asked, "Why say thanks to me?"

The voice had that crackle of amusement in it as it explained, "Well, it's people like you because of whom we got created. You give meaning to our existence." After that day, I never dared to speed up.

Yes, every entity wants to find meaning for its existence, including you and me, no?

UNTITLED #50

I know I am saying a lot. Can't hold my thoughts.

Take your time with what people call the 'right' time. Because what time can be the right time than the present moment?

The thought hit me as I was reading, thinking and wondering. It could be a repetition. Yes, it can be.

If my parents had not asked me to say Mama and Papa repeatedly, I would have never been able to address them with clear diction and the right words. They added to my childhood curiosity by constantly motivating me and pushing me to practice things. Ah, it's all about practice.

If we are negative today, carrying our doubts, fears, worries & anger, it is because we have practised doubting, worrying, fearing and getting angry. We can change all that by practising trust, faith, courage and patience. For that, one thing would be essential to understand and know: We can stop rejecting ourselves. The world will find ways to do that anyway. We have to accept ourselves exactly the way we are and then practice to become better. I repeat, then practice to become better. I am constantly practising.

You can too. Why not?

UNTITLED #51

Will you like to engage in a simple exercise today?

Getting Rid of Blame.

There was a time when I got into the habit of blaming everyone and everything else for my life condition, personal or professional life. Then another time came when I got into the process of working on myself to make corrections. I got in touch with Zen and started practising it in small ways. I was awestruck by the simplicity of learning it offered. It was actually kind of "a practice of returning YOU to Yourself". I realised that whenever I blamed someone, I was going away from myself. Now, both couldn't be practised together, returning to and going away from myself. So I decided to choose the latter. I consciously started a practice.

Whenever I found myself blaming external factors, my subconscious would make me do it. I would stop and send blessings to the persons I blamed and then look at how I was responsible and what contributed to that situation or condition. I would then take the necessary action. (It didn't felt easy initially but then it became easier with constant practice). This led to a slow and steady reduction of blame in my life. Have I eliminated it fully? Well, we are human beings. So shun blame; send blessings!

UNTITLED #52

We were sitting in a group and talking.

The topic of discussion was spiritual. One of my favourite topics.

An intense discussion was going on when suddenly someone who had not participated and was an acquaintance exploded for the reasons best known to him and, looking at me, He almost shouted: "What the hell do you think of yourself?"

I kept my calm and responded, "Nothing. And why are you thinking of me?" He gave me a strange look, found himself suddenly disarmed, didn't have the answer,

Yes, why should we think about others if it is not adding anything to our lives?

UNTITLED #53

He came from a good background and had a lot in him. However, organisations go by their set rules, and he was placed at the lowest level as he didn't fit the competency criteria. But, yes, he had his style and flair and also some air.

The meeting had gone well, and it was the first time. He had participated in a meeting in the absence of his boss. He was absolutely confident and candid in sharing his thoughts. Some people had found it difficult to appreciate given him being too junior to them. After the meeting, he came out and just stood looking up at the skies, a habit for aeons, perhaps.

That's when he found a senior executive tapping on his shoulder and almost shouting at him, showing angst,

"Damn it, boy, you talk like a GM."

He looked at him and spoke in an apologetic tone, "Oh, is it? I am sorry. I will improve."

The senior executive accepted the apology and felt good.

UNTITLED #54

Increments and promotions were being announced. My friend, a visitor and guest of the company's owners, was surprised to see the mixed emotions. Those emotions varied from being ecstatic to being absolutely broken. There was whispered criticism of the bosses for being biased.

What was the reason? My friend wondered.

Incidentally, he had to return the same evening. He happened to be travelling with one of the directors of the company. He asked the director, "Sir, despite good increments, why do people feel unhappy?

I felt some of the brighter ones appeared upset. What do bosses look at while assessing their people and deciding on rewards? "Well, the Director, a gentleman, shared this," Bosses always want performers, the go-getters, that is true. And generally, they take performance as guaranteed unless there are visible fluctuations.

Finally, they ask this one question - Can I depend on him/her? - well, a yes may make the person get more in comparison to another who may be brighter but less dependable. Others around, of course, won't appreciate this."

Dependability still matters even after so many decades.

UNTITLED #55

My colleague had just returned to the office after being on leave for a couple of days. She appeared sad and looked a bit low. When I inquired, she shared that she had lost a near one. She almost cried. Another colleague heard it and went out and shared the sad news with others. Meeting them teary-eyed, she was able to keep her poise.

After some time, the boss walked in and offered his condolences. Suddenly she couldn't control herself and cried as the tears flowed. Those were indeed very emotional moments. Our boss consoled her, and after he left, a colleague said, "You shouldn't have cried like a baby in front of the boss." She looked at him and replied, "Why? I wanted to cry, so I cried. I am not ashamed of my emotions."

Indeed, there would be occasions when one need not hold one's emotions to demonstrate inner strength.

I think expressing emotions when they need to be expressed makes one truly emotionally intelligent. And not otherwise. I had learned a lesson that day.

UNTITLED #56

As I was sitting on the chair to have my breakfast. I realised I needed to wash my hands.

I got up when my spouse said, "You washed them. You are lost somewhere." Obviously, I became absolutely focused and alive the next day as I was washing my hands. And this is what I experienced:

My hands are full of soap, and thousands of bubbles shine like tiny planets and stars; ah, a whole blinking universe!!

A gush of water and the universe goes.

I find myself looking at those lines on my palms, which looked like rivers of destiny crisscrossing, making strange patterns.

Oh, I was losing focus, so I returned and closed the tap, dried my hands softly and smelled the aroma the soap had left on my hands.

Listening to a melodious song being played on my mobile and walking towards the dining table, in my mind, I could taste the cookies. Suddenly everything felt beautiful.

UNTITLED #57

He was nine and on a school trip.

Divided into groups, they were directed to climb a mountain of moderate height. He started with the group and then suddenly took a lot of speed. He was gifted by God and, therefore, aimed to be the first to reach the top. He wanted to show off his ability and agility to his friends whom he had left behind.

Going up faster and faster, negotiating challenging terrain and turns, finally, he reached the top. A temple stood there. He found none around. He was alone. Suddenly, fear overtook him. The whistling sound of the wind added to that eerie feeling. He shouted to find someone, perhaps a priest or an attendant and didn't get a response.

He quietly sat on the staircase with his eyes closed to wait for his friends. He could hear his own heartbeat. How lonely he was feeling alone on the top!! A very scary experience.

A lesson was learnt. Since then, he has scaled many mountains and always took someone along. He continues to do so for every height he conquers. He never tries to reach the top alone. He is not able to forget that scary feeling. If you are on your way to the top, check if you have someone along. If not, find out one and hold hands. You will reach stronger.

UNTITLED #58

Do you think you are indispensable?

A simple way to check is this - Leave.

Promise me that you will not get upset if, after some time, even your echo from there refuses to respond.

Appears to be a dark thought, isn't it?

Trust me, nothing would ever offer brighter light of life lesson than passing through this one reality.

Therefore, hold hands, move forward together, and remember, whatever your ability, stature, or experience, someone is ready to take your place.

Be a contributor, and don't expect.

Indeed, humility is a shining trait of the 'contributors'.

UNTITLED #59

THEN:

People would join the organisation and not leave till retirement.

Loyalty to the organisation mattered.

A raw individual, on his first day, went to his boss to seek advice and ask if there were any suggestions for him to learn.

Boss looked at him and said, "I don't advise. I watch from a distance."

The young talent couldn't judge or understand. He quietly started giving his best. In three decades of association, he was never able to cover that distance.

When he shared this, I wondered what must have kept him for so many years there. He replied with one word, "Destiny..."

NOW:

In today's time, perhaps the youngster would have asked, "Why do you say that, sir and what will happen by keeping your distance?"

Boss would have fumbled, and the youngster would have left the organisation in about a week.

If I had asked him why he left the organisation so early, he would have said, "Well, I didn't like the attitude of the boss."

UNTITLED #60

"Hey RS, the world is moving very fast. You must also speed up. Adjust your values, go with the flow and see where your talent will take you. World wants embellishments and frills. Give them those. You will be applauded," Mr. XYZ was feeling concerned about me.

I am perceived as a bit slower by him because he thinks my strong conviction in certain work ethics holds me back and doesn't allow me to take risks. He sees me as stubborn and believes that a little compromise should be acceptable. He goes on to say, "People want teamwork in a resort; give it to them. They want 'Interpersonal skills' without 'Self Awareness', give them that; they want 'Professional Effectiveness' without 'Personal Effectiveness' first, give them that too." However, I don't agree with his views, as I believe I shouldn't.

So, I respond, "Let me be slow. I want to carry more sun and air in my heart along the journey and reach wherever I can by staying true to my path."

I am convinced that even someone involved in motor racing, which may be driving extremely fast, must also be consciously planning their win while sitting in quiet, thinking slowly so that they can think and act quickly when the moment demands it. Just a perspective.

UNTITLED #61

On a particular day in September 2019, I found myself feeling low. Out of my habit and practice, I decided to check out on the reason. I realised that I had let a small, disturbing thought enter my mind, I had to shift it…

I decided to get up and walk out to the balcony of our 11th-floor apartment. Standing straight, I consciously focused on my breathing and soon found myself witnessing a star-studded night, a brilliantly shining moon, a city illuminated by beautiful lights, a plane slowly descending with blinking lights, and cars driving on the highway with their headlights on. The entire scene added a magical sparkle to the night. As a cool breeze brushed against me, my heart filled with joy. Even the constant hum of the air conditioner began to sound like a rhythmic melody. Overwhelmed with happiness, the low feeling disappeared, and I stored this experience in my mind before going to sleep.

Today, I encountered a similar low feeling. Closing my eyes, I revisited the scene and experience I had saved in my mind from that night on the balcony. I saw it again and heard the sounds. To my surprise, my mood changed instantly. My mind couldn't distinguish between reality and imagination. This is just a glimpse of how NLP (Neuro-Linguistic Programming) can work for you.

UNTITLED #62

"Will you just keep your mouth shut" I shouted at him. And that's when I realised this is what I should have told me instead in my mind. It would have been totally different. Most of the time, what we want others to do, we fail in doing the same. And those are the moments when we need to reflect.

This thought leads me to another thought. All those like me who are in the profession of helping people develop a positive attitude, if we were to be assessed by our families, what would they tick out of the options here:

Always positive,

Often positive,

Sometimes positive,

Never positive.

What do I say? I can assure you one thing - it will NOT be a tick on "1" for me. Ha, Ha.

UNTITLED #63

About three decades ago, I found myself discussing my self-appraisal with my mentor. As he reviewed the ratings I had given myself for various traits, I felt a bit nervous. He suddenly paused, looked at me, and asked, "9/10 in Written Communication, Ramesh? Compared to whom?" I responded, "Sir, this is in comparison to my peers in the company." After all, I had been taught that surpassing classmates in school was a significant achievement.

He advised me, "I would like you to compare yourself with the best in the organisation." I was taken aback and asked him, "Sir, how would you rate yourself?" He replied, "5/10." His answer genuinely surprised me. I asked, "Sir, I consider you the best in the organisation, and you're giving yourself a 5? May I ask - compared to whom?"

He explained, "Compared to the editorials of The Times of India, my favourite." Feeling embarrassed, I said, "In that case, let it be 3/10 for me, sir." He smiled and told me, "I'm happy that you've realised. Remember, when it comes to self-appraisal, the only way to stay a learner is to compare yourself with the best, not just the best around you." This advice has served me well as I continually strive to learn, even though I am yet to reach the level of the best in anything.

UNTITLED #64

Do yourself a favour tonight. Indulge in this exercise.

Time SOTCO – Time spent thinking about correcting others.

Time SOTCS - Time spent thinking about correcting self.

Time SOTCO – Time SOTCS = (Reducing the number here every night will mean a happier life)

It has helped me. It will help you.

UNTITLED #65

I was invited by a company to deliver a training session at a 5-star hotel in Pune. To avoid any delays due to traffic, I arrived half an hour early and spent some time in the lounge browsing through books. Five minutes before the session was scheduled to begin, I contacted the organiser and was told to meet him at the main entrance of the banquet hall being used for the training, where he would come out to receive me. I went there and waited, admiring the beautiful paintings on the wall.

After waiting for a while, I called the organiser again. He said the previous session had just ended, and he would be out in a minute. Shortly after, a young man emerged from the door, seemingly looking for me, the trainer. He glanced at me but quickly looked away, scanning the rest of the area before shaking his head and returning to the room. I was puzzled by his actions.

So, I called him once more and said, "When you come out this time, don't expect the trainer to be 5'11" or 6', holding a tablet, and wearing trendy jeans and a T-shirt. Instead, look for a grey-haired, 5'4" man in an old blue blazer. That's me."

This time, he found me. Our minds often lead us to rely on our perceptions.

UNTITLED #66

As I gaze at the rising sun, I am captivated by the golden light splashing across the sky. I take a deep breath in and exhale slowly. As I breathe in, my heart whispers, "Life is beautiful," and as I breathe out, it affirms, "I am happy." However, my mind interrupts, "No, you can't be happy. Have you forgotten yesterday's turmoil? Remember that hurtful comment your friend made? You should be feeling hurt and angry, not happy and joyous."

My mind has brought the pain from the previous evening into the present. The subconscious has an uncanny habit of dredging up unwanted memories without warning. I need to cleanse it.

I reconnect with my conscious mind and repeatedly tell my heart, "Life is beautiful, and I am happy. It's a new day." Gradually, I start feeling good again, and the pain dissipates.

With a smile on my face, I notice everything around me seems to be smiling too. As I walk beneath an old oak tree, an extended branch appears to bless me. Overwhelmed with gratitude, I approach the tree and embrace it. As I turn around, I catch a glimpse of a fading figure of pain walking past me before it melts away and evaporates. I feel free and light.

UNTITLED #67

In 1986, I was someone with very strong likes and dislikes. One day, while riding on the back of a friend's motorcycle, I saw a person approaching from the opposite direction. I couldn't help but blurt out, "I dislike him."

My friend pulled over and asked, "Why do you dislike him?"

I pondered the question and replied, "Just like that. I don't know the reason. But I dislike him." My friend became somewhat irritated and said, "I don't understand this. How can you dislike a person without any reason?" He then shared a thought that has stayed with me ever since and has guided my life.

He asked, "If you can dislike a person without any reason, then why can't you like that person without any reason? Tell me!" I didn't have an answer, but the question made a lot of sense. He continued, "Your choices define you, not others. Disliking someone without a valid reason doesn't seem like a good choice."

Sadly, we lost my friend K.K. Shah many years ago, but his words have always lived on. Since then, I have found it very difficult to hate or dislike someone.

UNTITLED #68

GM: Alright, let's discuss who you're recommending for promotion. Let's finalise this.

Manager: Sir, I have two candidates: Mr R and Mr S.

GM: Tell me about them.

Manager: Sir, in my opinion, Mr R is excellent. He's highly self-motivated, and I never have to give him any instructions. He does what he should and sometimes even more.

GM: And what about Mr S?

Manager: Sir, he's also good, but he needs motivation. Once he's motivated, he performs well, if not better than Mr R. I actually like him. He may not be as sharp as Mr R, but with proper guidance, he seldom fails. He's very dependable, sir! Mr R is so self-driven that it sometimes scares me.

GM: So, wouldn't you like to boost Mr S's motivation by promoting him? That would be safer for you too. Mr R, being self-motivated, will find his way, and he's six months junior to Mr S, right?

Manager: Yes, sir, he is.

GM: Well then, it's settled.

Manager: Sir, should I officially recommend Mr S for promotion?

GM: Yes, let's do it.

(Is this fiction or non-fiction? That's for you to decide.)

UNTITLED #69

A new supervisor with strong technical acumen and conceptual ability was assigned to oversee two experienced workers on the shop floor. However, he lacked extensive experience. At one point during an operation, the workers encountered a problem. The supervisor assessed the issue and suggested a slight tweak to the process to achieve the desired outcome. The workers, having decades of experience, did not appreciate his input and believed themselves to be more competent. This particular task had been assigned by the boss.

For an hour, no progress was made. The supervisor tried his best to persuade the workers, but they refused to listen. The boss's phone was switched off during this time. Eventually, the boss came to check on the status of the operation. The workers informed him about the problem they were facing. After carefully examining the issue, the boss provided a solution that was identical to what the supervisor had suggested an hour earlier. The supervisor couldn't help but say, "This is exactly what I've been telling them. They didn't listen to me, and we wasted an hour of valuable time." He expected the boss to reprimand the workers.

Instead, the boss looked at the supervisor and asked, "Are you saying that you can think like me?"

UNTITLED #70

I fondly remember those days when I would meditate on the rising sun in a beautiful garden every morning.

During those moments of meditation, I needed nothing and noticed nothing. I transcended beyond my body and simply existed. I became a living prayer, flowing with the rhythm of my own breath. That state of pure happiness was something I cherished. Even when work awaited me, and opportunities to justify my existence smiled at me, I remained in that constant state of happiness. I made subtle, positive differences in the lives of others without even realising it. I faced life's storms without acknowledging them as storms, and I embraced each moment for what it was.

In uncontrollable moments, I experienced happiness in various emotions: anger, sadness, upset, tearfulness, and hurt. I always returned to that joyous state of happiness, living in a meditative state. After a couple of years, I have now restarted this practice.

Now, I know - as you do - what truly brings happiness. Your work and the values you uphold will make you happy. If you can make a subtle, positive difference in someone's life without causing harm to others or yourself through your actions or thoughts, you will find happiness. Why wouldn't you?

UNTITLED #71

"Why are you crying?" the little one asked me as I sat alone on a bench, watching the sunset.

"I'm upset. I can't think positively; my mind is filled with negative thoughts. I feel so helpless."

"Why do you want to feel helpless? Forget about your mind. Use your heart to think."

A cool breeze brushed my face as the waves of the sea gently kissed my feet. I suddenly felt light and comfortable. All my stress washed away as I listened to the rocks laugh with every wave that crashed against them.

I realised that I had already started thinking with my heart. I wanted to thank the little ones, but they were nowhere to be found. Was it all just a figment of my imagination? I've never been able to solve that puzzle. However, one thing is certain - within a few days, my mind was freed from most of the negativity. My heart and mind began working together, knowing when not to merge as one. There are moments when their conflict prevents me from slipping further into negativity.

UNTITLED #72

In 1982, I sat on a train, gazing out the window as the journey began. I was leaving behind the city of my birth, my friends, and my childhood. With tears in my eyes, I felt a wave of sadness. The older man sitting next to me noticed and asked, "Why are you crying? What happened?" I looked at him and replied, "I'm leaving my city forever. I've lost everything."

He stared at me and questioned, "Everything?" I responded, "Yes, everything. Nothing is left."

"But something brought you to this train, didn't it?" he continued. "Yes, the hope that somewhere, someplace, I'll find a new life."

"I can see that your confidence has stayed with you as well. Remember, nothing is truly lost. You still have everything. Hope and confidence, these twins, will take you to new places. So smile, feel blessed, and all the best!" With that, he stood up to disembark. He was an angel sent by God at the right time and place. I was too overwhelmed to ask for his name or occupation. I watched him walk along the platform towards the exit.

I smiled, and that smile has remained with me ever since. I may not have gone to numerous places, but I am here in this space, happily sharing and learning alongside you. Thank you!

UNTITLED #73

As we watched Mr X walking towards us, my friend mumbled, "He thinks he's so great."

Surprised, I responded, "But right now, you're thinking that he thinks he's great. That's your thought, not his."

Before my friend could reply, Mr X approached us, and my friend smiled broadly, exclaiming, "Wow, it's so nice to see you! Welcome!"

It seemed that my friend had just demonstrated how we tend to be nicer to those we criticise behind their backs. So, it's essential not only to check ourselves for such behaviour but also to be cautious of those who are overly kind to us.

In 2002, I wrote the following verse in my book, inspired by a thought from Hugh Prather:

"I do despise, dislike, and hate you,

I cherish talking against you.

But isn't it strange that when we meet,

It's always me who is first to greet..."

Take a moment to reflect on your own behaviour, and keep in mind to be wary of those who are excessively nice to you. Because, deep down, you know the truth.

UNTITLED #74

My morning walks have always been magical, filled with delightful and joyful experiences. About a year ago, while walking through my usual route, a senior friend whispered to me as he passed by, "The sky is clear and blue; take some Sun home with you."

I obliged. I captured some sunlight in my eyes, a bit on my face, and a little in my heart. This morning, I remembered that incident, and as the environment was similar, with a crystal-clear sky and the sun rising, I did the same. I gathered some Sun as I walked. I know that my words will appear happier and brighter as I share some of this sunlight with you. May you pick up a bit of sun here and let your face glow with a sunny smile.

UNTITLED #75

He stopped me on the way and said, "Sir, your session inspired me. I will quit smoking."

"Have you already started?" I asked.

He had participated in a short two-hour session on Positive Attitude the previous week.

"No, sir, I've resolved to quit on my birthday - June 1st," he said excitedly.

Well, he was waiting for a special day to start working on his health. It's not about resolutions; it's about attitude. If I'm aware of behaviours, habits, or relationships that are unhealthy for me, I can't wait for a special day to free myself from their control. Once you see a tiny insect in your cup of tea, you don't wait. You stop drinking that tea.

Any bad habit is like an insect in the cup of life. You can't keep living without removing it. So, let's get started NOW for a happier, better life.

UNTITLED #76

I was going down from the 10th floor of a residential complex where a friend lived, and the elevator stopped on the first floor. A young man, about 20, dressed in a tracksuit and holding a bag, entered. I struck up a conversation and asked why he was dressed like that. He replied, "I'm going to the gym, sir. You know, fitness matters, right?" Well, he was correct. The elevator came to a halt, the door opened, and as I stepped out, I asked him, "Is that why you took the elevator to go down from the first floor?"

Did I receive an answer? Oh no, as you might have guessed, he didn't have one.

UNTITLED #77

When you can't find the key in its usual spot in the drawer and can't locate it elsewhere, you return to the same drawer, murmuring, "It has to be there..." You open it once more, forgetting that the key isn't there. You're unsure of what prompts you to do this, unaware of what triggered your action.

Reflecting on the past, you'll realise that there have been many instances when you acted without knowing why. Accepting this truth will be a transformative moment in your life, and you'll love it.

This self-realisation is as addictive as ignorance.

UNTITLED #78

Here's a straightforward test to determine if you're a good manager: Would you like or prefer your son/daughter to work under a manager like you? During my time in the corporate world, there were moments when my answer to this question would be 'yes,' and at other times, it would be 'no.' If you can honestly answer with a resounding YES, then people should seek opportunities to work with you.

UNTITLED #79

He approached me with a legitimate excuse: Sir, I couldn't complete the task you assigned me because I couldn't find the time.

My advice was straightforward: Instead of focusing on how to find time to do what you want to do, consider what you can STOP doing. This way, you'll free up ample time, enabling you to accomplish what you need to do.

UNTITLED #80

"Excuse me, sir, I need your time."

"Why? I thought we all had the same amount of time."

"No, I want your time for myself."

"Oh, that means I won't be able to use that time for myself. Well, I can give you my time. Of course. But what would I get in return?"

"Sir, I don't understand."

"I mean, compensate me for the time I give you." He hung up the phone.

UNTITLED #81

I stopped at a petrol station. Rolling down the window, the attendant asked, "How much, sir? Can you give me the keys, please?"

I handed over the keys and said, "Fill it with Rs.1000 worth of petrol."

He filled the tank, returned the keys, and I gave him the money.

As he handed back the keys and accepted the payment, he smiled brightly and said, "Thanks a lot, sir!" His smile shone as darkness slowly descended. I knew at that moment that I would stop by again next time.

Consider this - we have numerous interactions daily where there is a transaction between us and someone else. Yet, we often fail to smile or say thanks. If you disagree, think about your transactions with your spouse or a friend in the last 24 hours. I'm sure a few of those transactions deserved to conclude with a smile and a thank you but didn't. Alas! What do you think?

Let me say thank you with a smile. You received what I transacted, and that has made my day. Now, don't keep the smile to yourself. Pass it on to someone else.

UNTITLED #82

I remember as a child when I would suddenly wake up in the middle of the night, I would hear watchmen shouting in Hindi, "Jaagatey Raho," telling their counterparts nearby to stay awake. It served as a warning for thieves and other wrongdoers to stay away, making people feel safe.

Today, for this space and vicinity, I changed these words and shouted out loud - "Seekhtey Raho," encouraging everyone to keep learning. In this world where digital flows impact every aspect of our lives, the only safety net for us is learning. Make time to learn and keep pace. You must stay updated. When was the last time you learned something new about your own field?

UNTITLED #83

It happened on a particular morning. I saw him walking towards me as we crossed paths during my morning walk, just like we did every day. My attempts to greet him had always failed, as he never even glanced at me. Trust me, I find it extremely difficult not to acknowledge someone, even on the first occasion. I may not say hello, but I will definitely look at the person for a moment and, depending on the exchange, offer a smile before moving on. However, some people find it very easy to overlook or ignore others. Despite this, I decided to call out and greet him. As he came closer, I said, "Good Morning!" He seemed flustered at first but then composed himself, forming a smile and responding, "Good Morning!" We continued on our way.

Things pleasantly changed next morning. He looked at me from a distance, and by the time he reached me, there was already a smile and a cheerful exchange of "Good Morning."

We introduced ourselves within a couple of days. It feels good to interact with those whom you pass by every day. We live in a time when even a simple greeting can be risky. We've become accustomed to doubting everyone around us. Let's start practising trust, and a greeting could be a good beginning.

UNTITLED #84

He said, "Sir, I'm not confident. It seems like life isn't being fair to me."

I listened, looked into his eyes, and asked, "You started by sending me a message that you wanted to talk to me, right?"

"Yes, sir, because I thought you could help me."

"So, you were confident in sending me that message?" I asked with a questioning tone.

"Sir, initially, I was hesitant. But as I read more of your posts, I decided to reach out."

"You decided to be confident in asking me?" I questioned again.

He thought about it and said, "Yes!"

"Then is it possible for you to decide to be confident in other situations too? You can start small. Where would you like to decide to be confident next?"

"Sir, I'd like to talk to my boss about changing my work."

"So, go ahead."

"Sir, what if he says no?"

"Then change confidently," I smiled.

"Oh, thank you so much, sir. I get it."

I hope he understands more of it... Life is simple. We make it complicated.

UNTITLED #85

A child was playing with an expensive, delicate toy in the park, indicating that he came from wealthy parents. As it often happens, he broke the toy. His mother yelled at him, "Why did you break it?" In all his innocence, he replied, "You were the one who gave it to me. It broke. What can I do? You shouldn't have given it to me." The child didn't want to be blamed for the loss. No one likes to be blamed.

UNTITLED #86

"Can't you understand? I'm so angry with you that I don't even look at you when we pass each other in the evenings. Can't you tell?"

I didn't know why he was talking like that. Someone being angry at me without my knowledge, for reasons known only to them, can't really be a concern for me.

And if I have to worry about him not looking at me, I won't because of this:

Whenever I've avoided someone for a specific reason, I've always found it necessary to think about them and picture them in my mind. By doing this, in a way, I'm actually honouring those people.

UNTITLED #87

The young person asked the elder sitting with him in the lounge, "Sir, I wonder how people like us will survive in this rapidly changing world. Our learning speed seems slower than the rate of change, causing a lot of stress. What advice would you give to students like us?"

The elder thought and replied, "Well, you need to improve your speed. There's nothing else that can be done. And that will happen only if you use every available moment to learn. Only you can decide how to do it and what you need to stop doing to find time." Saying this, the elder went back to checking his mobile for new Facebook messages about where his friends ate, what movies they saw, and if there was any fresh teasing.

What do you think - Did the student start looking for ways to make time for learning immediately?

UNTITLED #88

Around fifteen years ago, when I was in the corporate sector, I experienced a significant learning moment.

A short circuit led to an air conditioner in a senior executive's cabin catching fire. As an HR representative, I quickly rushed to the scene. Since it was a window AC, some people were pouring water and sand from the outside. That's when I grabbed a fire extinguisher and bravely entered the smoke-filled room to try to put out the fire. Fortunately, the fire was quickly extinguished, possibly due to the efforts from the other side of the wall. However, I felt suffocated and emerged coughing. I was taken to the hospital and given medication to cleanse my system since I had inhaled some smoke.

The next morning, the Managing Director called a meeting to review the causes and discuss the preventive measures needed. He praised the efforts of some individuals, and I eagerly awaited appreciation. Then, he turned to me and scolded me for my reckless actions without taking necessary precautions, such as covering my nose and mouth with a wet cloth. He was furious. I have never forgotten that lesson and the manner in which it was delivered. The ignorant had been praising me while wisdom had struck hard.

UNTITLED #89

I used to frequently walk on the footpath along Karve Road in Pune during my evenings when we lived in that area.

One day, I was walking quite fast and soon found myself in sync with another person, a complete stranger. At that moment, a young boy parking his bike at the edge of the road caught my eye as I passed by him, and I turned to look back. I couldn't quite place him as I continued walking. Then I turned again, looking behind me, but I still couldn't remember his name. He seemed like someone I knew from the past. After two attempts, I decided to focus on my walk. That's when I noticed that the person walking almost next to me had moved quite far ahead.

At that moment, I realised that looking back had significantly slowed me down. It truly had. From that day on, I have always focused on moving forward. I only look back if compelled by my inner state of mind when I'm relaxing or sitting idle, which is rare. Otherwise, looking ahead has kept me in good shape and propelled me forward at a nice pace. It was much later that I watched the movie Bhaag Milkha Bhaag, and the first scene showed Milkha losing the race because he looked back, losing his momentum.

UNTITLED #90

The sun rose quietly, and an excited butterfly gazed at the rose. It was a very sincere look. The rose responded by slowly opening up. The butterfly, fluttering her wings with dreams in her eyes, prepared herself to meet the rose. That's when a couple of tiny, laughing fingers snapped at the rose and plucked it. Neither the butterfly nor I, as a silent observer, were amused. However, the little girl struck by poverty, wearing a tattered frock adorned with a pattern of joyous colourful flowers, didn't seem to care. She had found her moment of happiness in a real rose.

The butterfly turned and fluttered her wings, flying away in search of another one.

I don't know anything about the rose's feelings, but I am sure that it must have released all its fragrance to make the little girl feel better. After all, it had come into existence to spread its fragrance. It must have done so for whatever moments it had.

After reflecting on this, I felt there was a hidden lesson for all of us. Perhaps we could aim to live a purposeful life for at least some moments during each day. What do you think?

UNTITLED #91

Every morning, I like to imagine that I am born again. I just think about it, and then I wonder what would happen if I could practice some of the pure traits of an infant every day:

I would find myself free from all the darker emotions; I would stay curious to learn from everything and everyone I come in contact with. I would not be eager to know anything about tomorrow or remember anything about yesterday. I would simply live in the present. I would receive whatever I needed. I would eat when hungry and sleep when tired, just like a Zen Master. I would laugh and cry whenever I felt like it, without any set rules. I would gaze at the Moon and touch it by releasing a balloon from my little fingers. Oh, what a wonderful feeling that would be!

UNTITLED #92

She was sitting with me in a coffee shop, sipping her coffee. Everything seemed normal and relaxed. We were meeting to discuss a problem she had, and she needed my advice. Suddenly, her face contorted as she angrily whispered, "I hate her. I don't know why she should be here at this time..." I looked at her. She seemed genuinely upset, and her mood had changed entirely. For quite some time, she kept glancing towards that other 'friend' of hers and remained agitated. I asked her, "How can you shift from such a calm mood to a disturbed mood so quickly? I need to learn. With me, it's always the reverse. I quickly return to a good mood from a bad one. I must learn to reverse it too. Wow, going from a good mood to a bad mood!"

"What do you mean?" she appeared flustered and confused. "No, you did something to change your mood, right? What did you do?" "Why would I do anything? It just happened." "Still, you did something, didn't you?" "No. It just happened unconsciously," she almost snapped at me. It's interesting how things happen without our awareness. We give so much power to some people over us without them ever knowing that merely thinking about them takes away joy from our own precious moments, created with conscious effort. Then we say - We don't need training in self-awareness.

UNTITLED #93

I've been pondering something for the past few days, and I must confess that whenever I hear people talk about "learn-unlearn-learn," I feel uneasy. From my understanding, if I have learned something, I can never unlearn it unless I experience some kind of brain injury that causes my neurons to shift their position or break certain neural networks. However, I can learn improved versions or new things and decide to stop using what I had learned earlier. To emphasise, I can choose not to use my previous knowledge.

For example, when I learned to drive a motorcycle, I didn't unlearn how to ride a bicycle. Similarly, when I learned to drive a car, I didn't unlearn how to ride a motorcycle. If necessary, I could ride a bicycle again. So why do we keep creating phrases like "learn-unlearn-learn" just because we want to?

UNTITLED #94

Some lessons stay with us for a lifetime.

At 22, I left my luxurious life as part of a business family and joined a corporation in 1982, whether by choice or necessity. As I started working, I realised that my background, filled with a hint of arrogance and a sense of superiority, would become a significant concern for both my bosses and me.

Being a loudmouth, on my second day in the department, I asked a fellow staff member about his work in the office. He told me about a very routine task that could be considered drudgery. I laughed at him and ridiculed the work he was doing. He was upset but didn't show it.

The next morning, the scene changed: I was standing in front of my boss, and he assigned me the same task I had mocked.

I couldn't protest because I wasn't in a position to do so. I spent the next six years doing that job.

After that experience, I never mocked anyone for the work they were doing. I learned that every person and every role is essential in an organisation, as each contributes to the larger goal in some way.

UNTITLED #95

Despite honking continuously, the car ahead didn't make room for me, and when I tried to maneuver from the right side, another car driving parallel wouldn't budge. No one was giving me space, and I felt trapped. It was so irritating! However, I couldn't stay in that emotional state and eventually surrendered.

This situation prompted me to reflect on how people around me must feel when I don't give them space.

I learned from that experience a few years ago. Life has improved since then. I believe people no longer feel suffocated in my presence and can find ample room to breathe.

UNTITLED #96

He glanced at me and asked, "Show me how things work in your place."

So, I began explaining.

We couldn't make any progress. Why, you ask?

Because he wanted to understand by seeing things, while I insisted on making him understand by listening about them... Haha!

UNTITLED #97

My first encounter with creativity occurred when I needed to iron my trousers for a classmate's birthday party. However, due to a power outage in the summer of 1973, using an electric iron was not an option.

Yet, the creative child in me noticed a steel cooking utensil with a flat surface at the bottom. I had an idea. Electric irons had a flat steel surface, and this utensil had a similar surface. I figured if I could heat the bottom of the utensil, it should work like an iron. So, I placed the utensil directly on the gas stove's burning flames while I was home alone. When I felt the utensil was hot enough, I picked it up with tongs and pressed the trousers with its flat surface. To my surprise, the trousers were ruined, leaving me with shorts unfit for the occasion.

Thanks to my scientifically innovative mind, I had turned myself into a caricature. That memory still brings a smile to my face, reminding me of my innocent and creative childhood. I continued to follow that spark of creativity, and now I can smooth out the worry lines on people's foreheads through engaging and refreshing conversations in my training and coaching sessions.

UNTITLED #98

Today, something made me pause. In the early morning, a couple of words in a newspaper headline caught my eye: "Save Planet." I wondered, who are we to save the planet? It has sustained itself for the past 6.5 billion years, and I'm sure it will continue to do so for another 6.5 billion years. The real question is whether 'life' that evolved over aeons can save itself or not. To put it another way, can 'humanity' accelerate its efforts to protect all forms of "life" on the planet? Let's remember that life on Earth is not just about humans like you, me, and everyone else. It also includes the myriad forms of life on land, in the sea, and in the sky.

Thomas Friedman expressed this idea beautifully in his recent book "Thanks for Being Late." I have simply conveyed it in my own straightforward way. I think a slogan like "Save Planet" doesn't immediately inspire a sense of responsibility in people, as they may feel insignificant and look to leaders to work towards the goal. All these thoughts crossed my mind as I walked. I looked up, and it seemed as if future generations were pleading from the skies: "Please leave some fresh air for us; save, plant, and nurture more trees!"

UNTITLED #99

"Sir, I joined this organisation thinking there wouldn't be any politics. I remember my father talking about the dirty games people played to pull others down during his time. I thought things had changed. How can we handle this?" he asked me. If only he had realised that everything on the planet could change, but emotions will always remain the same. I needed to respond, so I recalled the wise words of a senior executive who had addressed this crucial topic.

I told him, "We must consistently perform with all our talent because that's what the organisation expects from us. At the same time, we should accept politics as a natural phenomenon, just like the weather. We protect ourselves in harsh weather conditions, and we should learn to do the same when politics reveals its ugly side."

"But sir, what if it comes like a tsunami?""In that case, what can we do? We surrender. If we survive, we need to assess what's left and use everything we have to continue our existence. The tsunami of politics can't kill you; it can only throw you off-balance or leave you stranded." He asked, "Sir, what about you? Could you protect yourself?" That question caught me off guard. I dodged it, saying, "We're not talking about me, are we?"

UNTITLED #100

The Shatabdi Express arrived in Pune at 12:30 am, an hour late that day. I exited the station and took an auto-rickshaw. Out of habit, I struck up a conversation with the driver:

"What time do you go home? It's already 12:45 am," I asked.

"Sir, I'll return around 4:00 am." "Why do you drive at night?"

"Sir, during the day, I work as a helper in a company." "What are the hours?"

"Sir, 9:00 am to 6:00 pm." "When do you rest?"

"Sir, I sleep from 4:15 am to 7:30 am and then from 7:30 pm to 10:30 pm after having an early dinner. I start driving again at 11:00 pm."

"Why put in so much effort?"

"Sir, I have a son and a daughter. I want them to attend good schools and receive a proper education so they can succeed. The fees these days are so high! I have to do this for them. I earn more at night, which is another reason, sir."

"God bless you and your children!" I said.

As I thought about our conversation, I wondered about the concept of work-life balance. Would a session on work-life balance have helped him? It's incredible how contextual everything is!

UNTITLED #101

"You seem to be in love with yourself," I commented.

"Yes, I am because I've created reasons for that through constant work on myself."

This realisation struck me: if I wanted to love myself and, in turn, love others, I needed to create the right reasons for that.

It was crucial for me to determine which actions or thoughts would make me enjoy my own company. This revelation opened up new possibilities, and I felt my heart grow wings, ready to explore the vast skies of my inner space.

Believe me, it's not that difficult to make such a resolution. I also discovered that unless I liked my 'self' for the right reasons, it would be challenging to like others.

Consider this: you stopped here to read this inspiring quote. Something so positive. You made the right choice. At this moment, you have every reason to like yourself. So, smile, pat yourself on the back, feel good, and share the light with others. Before you sleep, remember to acknowledge all the right things you did today to like yourself. Give yourself one more pat, sleep, and wake up tomorrow to do even more. Life transforms just like that!

UNTITLED #102

It was sometime in the mid-nineties when I developed a routine of meditating at sunrise. I would find a spot where I could watch the sunrise and let the first sunbeams wash my face. Regardless of the city I visited, I would wake up early, find local transportation, and head to the city's sunrise point.

I remember the day I travelled on a night train from Pune to Khandwa with a senior executive. The train arrived in Khandwa around 5:10 am. I had mentioned my desire to find a sunrise point. We searched for a hotel for the next 15 minutes but were unsuccessful. I surrendered to the situation, praying silently.

Eventually, we found a hotel. It was about 5:40 am, and despite my suggestion to share a room and save money, my senior requested two separate rooms. The attendant led me to my room, opened it, and placed my luggage inside. I noticed two more doors. The boy opened one facing south, revealing the sky and scattered clouds. At that moment, I opened the other door on the eastern side. To my surprise, there was a large terrace, and right in front of me, at the edge of the wall, was the big red circle of the rising sun. Nothing stood between us. I sat down, and the sun and I connected. It was one of many small miracles I've experienced.

UNTITLED #103

I vividly recall attending an HR forum where there was a session on "Employee Retention." After everyone had asked their questions, the program coordinator handed me the cordless microphone and said, "Mr Ramesh, one question from you." I was puzzled and asked, "Why would you want me to ask?" She replied, "I know my participants and what they need." I felt obligated to honour her trust in me, so I turned to the speaker and asked, "As HR professionals, you're discussing employee retention in your respective organisations. But what about our own retention?"

Before the speaker could respond, a young executive, who appeared to be around 26 – the same number of years I had spent in HR at that point – turned to me and asked, "Are you anti-HR or something?" She was questioning me, someone who had lived and breathed HR. However, it's natural for things to change, and certain principles should remain constant. I decided not to respond to her, and the speaker chose not to answer my question.

My question was never addressed, but I still believe it was relevant. What do you think?

UNTITLED #104

Three things that will motivate me to prioritise buying from you, with other factors coming later:

1. How do I feel the moment I enter your premises? If I feel good for any reason, let me tell you, I've already become 50% your customer.
2. Do I find you confident when I ask product-related questions? Or do I hear an overconfident, eager-to-sell voice? A realistic evaluation of your product will instill confidence in you as a person of value.
3. Are you willing to go the extra mile to reveal any negative aspects of the product that may be hidden from plain sight? Being open about this will make me trust you more.

As a salesperson, you should know that the most crucial point is at the top of this list. To achieve this, you can learn some fundamentals about building rapport instantly. NLP (Neuro-Linguistic Programming) is an excellent resource for this, or you can choose any other intervention. However, mastering these three things is essential so that the rest can follow.

UNTITLED #105

He shared his story with me, explaining why he left his job - a terrible boss, an awful company, and poor prospects. I asked him, "So what are you going to do now?" He replied, "I'm becoming a Trainer. I've already pitched my idea." Naturally curious, I asked, "So what will you train people on?" He didn't hesitate, "Leadership or Personality Development! I have a couple of friends in high places, very close friends. They told me to do it, and they would help me with assignments." I probed further, "How will you create your modules? Have you ever led people?" He was indeed a confident person, "Sir, everything is available on the Internet. One just has to Google it. Easy. Having studied in a convent, English is not a problem." Suddenly, he asked me, "What do you do, sir?" I smiled and said, "I think."

I didn't want to feel embarrassed discussing my profession, which I had spent almost a lifetime achieving, while he only needed a Google search and a couple of friends. Sometimes, one needs to hold back in certain moments. We are all on our chosen paths. Some achieve external heights, others inner depths, and a rare few achieve both. I don't belong there. I am still constructing my wings for the flights to those glorious, unending skies of my inner space. My wings are not yet complete.

UNTITLED #106

Unexpectedly, I received a message from one of my young LinkedIn connections asking if he could meet me during his visit to Pune to discuss something. I agreed, and we met. After some initial small talk, our conversation shifted to what he wanted to know.

"Sir, I lack self-motivation." "How do you know that?"

"Sir, I'm not a self-motivating person. I've always needed a push from outside."

"So, did you write to me because someone pushed you?" "No, sir, I've been reading your posts, and I thought I would approach you. So, I did."

"That means you do have some degree of self-motivation. Now you're sitting with me after travelling for almost an hour in the city. Right?"

"Yes, sir!"

"So, you do have a good degree of self-motivation to do what you want to do. Isn't that right?"

He paused, thought it over, and said, "Right, sir!"

"Now, use that motivation for things you HAVE to do. You can do it. Just choose to do it. It's like picking up a chair from one place and putting it where you need it. The chair is available, but you're not looking at alternative uses. The same goes for motivation. You have it. Use it in other areas. And relax."

UNTITLED #107

I am all for Hard Work. I have always felt that our moms had to really work very hard to bring us up in earlier years of our childhood to give us the life that we have. So negating a little hard work to make our lives better only means we are negating her efforts. Think about it..

UNTITLED #108

The alarm blares, and he wakes up with a start, feeling groggy. He yawns and tells himself, "It's okay. I'll start tomorrow. Let me go back to my beauty sleep..."

And just like that, within minutes, he's snoring again.

Without hesitation, we often postpone doing what's good and perhaps essential for us. Yet, time doesn't wait; minutes continue to pass at the same speed. Instead of feeling fully alive, we feel sluggish during moments when we should be ready to conquer the world.

Let's make an effort to wake up each morning with a spring in our step, possibly even without an alarm. No more groggy, yawning moments. Let life be interesting and more meaningful. The day will reveal many beautiful gifts. Let's be ready to receive them by being fully present in every moment.

Just think – haven't you already started feeling better?

UNTITLED #109

"I can promise to be sincere, but I cannot promise to be impartial."

— Johann Wolfgang Von Goethe

This is my all-time favourite quote for a clear and deeply honest expression.

I remember a senior executive telling me that he was very impartial to the people in his team. He preferred no one. I heard him and casually asked, "I have heard a lot about your team members. All are really good. Who is your favourite?"

He was spontaneous, "I like S most."

UNTITLED #110

"How many stories do you still have to share?" His tone wasn't casual.

"Oh, plenty of them."

"How can you have so many?"

"Well, every interaction gives me a story.""What story can you take from our interaction?"

"Let's see. I might get one. Let me ask you a question - How did you choose the tone with which you asked me that question?"

"I don't know. I didn't even notice. It just happened."

"You could have asked me in an appreciative tone, right? You could have said - Wow, you write well. Will you keep sharing, please, as I want to learn more? - isn't it?"

"That's what I actually meant," his voice was weak.

"No, you didn't. Your tone gave it away. You were sarcastic." I was candid.

He sat quietly for some time and confessed, "Yes, my tone was not good. I agree. Somewhere deep inside, I envy you. Isn't that such a common emotion?"

"Yes, it is! However, acceptance makes you so special and unique. Doesn't it? It's a big thing to say - I envy you."

He smiled. I asked him, "So, do I have a story now? Tell me."

"Yes, you do."

UNTITLED #111

"You know, I can stay alone on a mountain. Somehow, I don't need people around to spend my time."

"But aren't you in sales? You need your customers, right?"

"Of course, but aren't they more than just 'people'? They're my customers," he raised his hand above his head to emphasise their importance.

It didn't surprise me at all when I learned that he was among the top performers in his company.

UNTITLED #112

I remember how my inquisitive mind often got me into trouble at school. I recall my English teacher saying, "We must keep bad people at arm's length." My curiosity compelled me to raise my hand and ask a question. With her permission, I inquired, "Whose arm's length, Ma'am?" She seemed taken aback by my question. I can still picture her expression etched in my memory. She composed herself and replied, "Yours." I wondered and asked again, "But what if the bad people have longer arms than me?" She couldn't answer, and after that, she never stopped me from raising my hand, which had a habit of going up during confusing moments.

Many years later, after being hurt by people with longer arms than me, I found the answer. I learned that we need to keep ourselves at "harm's length" from others. This distance ensures that no one can harm us. It makes a lot of sense, and now I can do it quite well.

I realised that we can avoid a lot of trouble if we don't embrace the 'cactuses' walking among us. We can respect them for who they are and admire their resilience and strength from a safe distance – at 'harm's length.'

UNTITLED #113

"RS, I want to feel powerful for at least a few moments every day."

I listened, considered his words, and responded, "There's a significant difference between feeling powerful and being powerful."

He seemed puzzled, paused, and said, "You know, I'm not even able to feel powerful because my actions are always under scrutiny. I'll be content with feeling powerful, even if it's just for a few moments."

An idea came to mind, "Try this: When you go home, and your spouse starts watching her favourite show on TV, quietly sit with her and hold the remote. You'll feel powerful in those moments, as you'll have the power to change the channel. Just feel it."

"Oh, it's so simple. I never thought about it."

I warned him, however, "Just know that you can and feel good about it. But don't actually change the channel, or you'll see the power shift in seconds."

This situation is quite common. When I was working, I noticed something peculiar. Bosses would delegate authority to their subordinates and encourage them to proceed, yet they would expect them not to use that power without first seeking approval. If you ever exercised that authority, you might receive praise from others, but it would mean making your boss a permanent enemy.

UNTITLED #114

When I was about 10 years old, my mom told me I could play any game or sport, but swimming was strictly off-limits. One day, without telling anyone, my older cousin took me to the swimming pool near our home.

He led me into the water, and I enjoyed it. It was so much fun. Then he asked me to close my eyes and hold my breath. Following his instructions, he took me deeper into the water until we were completely submerged. It felt incredibly light and exhilarating. After about a minute, despite wanting to stay underwater, I needed to breathe. So, I nudged my cousin with my elbow, our prearranged signal to resurface. In a few moments, we were back up, and I had an unforgettable experience. It was the last time I ever entered a swimming pool, as a neighbour informed my mom.

Why did I share this story? I've been reflecting on my life to understand the origins of my lessons. This incident demonstrated one thing very clearly: my life depended on making decisions based on my needs rather than my wants.

I realised that this principle should be the foundation for all decisions. So, the only decision one needs to make is to prioritise a 'need' over a 'want' when time is limited.

UNTITLED #115

I used to be a very aggressive table tennis player, and my behaviour often reflected that.

In August 1979, I arrived at the club and discovered that I had been overlooked for the district team for some reason. I was upset and angry. In my fury, I confronted the person responsible and insulted him. He was a senior member, and in his anger, he splashed water from the glass he was holding onto my face. I held a grudge against him for a long time.

Fast forward to 1994, when I read Dr Wayne Dyer's "You'll See It When You Believe It." The chapter on forgiveness intrigued me, and I decided that if I wanted my life to flow smoothly, I needed to seek forgiveness from those I had hurt in the past. I made a list of 10 people, including the man who had thrown water on my face.

Tracking him down after more than a decade, taking his hands, and asking for his forgiveness in a clear and confident voice was one of the most beautiful experiences of my life. He was overwhelmed, as he never expected such an encounter.

UNTITLED #116

Good thing about being a boss is:

You can say anything when you have your team around you and get away with it.

Bad thing about being a boss is:

You say it.

UNTITLED #117

A senior executive confessed,

"RS, I fear nurturing fresh talent with so many head-hunters around."

My answer was:

"If that's how it is, then Head Hunters won't have to find them. They will get found by the hunters."

UNTITLED #118

I was standing in a corner at Colaba Causeway behind the Taj in Mumbai during one of my visits, waiting for my cab. A constant stream of people flowed into the shopping paradise, where small vendors competed with designer showrooms. The contrast on display was evident in sight, sound, and feeling. Little did I know I would soon experience a striking similarity amid the contrasts.

Lost in thoughts, a balloon brushed my cheek, and I noticed a child living in poverty holding a couple of balloons gifted to him by a generous visitor. The boy had a beautiful smile as he stood at the edge of the road. At that moment, a Mercedes slowed down at the turn, and a child of similar age looked out the window, spotted the balloons, and flashed a beautiful smile at the less fortunate boy. The smile was warmly reciprocated with equal spirit. Two different worlds, two different children, yet their souls shared the same colour, as their smiles originated from the same depths of their inner beings.

I found myself smiling as well, praying for both of them. May the colour of their souls never change, and their smiles never lose their spontaneity.

UNTITLED #119

"We can empty our cup", – Zen saying

Indeed, we can. The moment I realized this, I began to slowly empty my cup because I needed to receive in order to give.

As I did so, I discovered that there were good things already in the cup. So, I decided to keep those things and not let the cup become entirely empty.

Happiness lies in giving and receiving in an ongoing cycle. Happiness can be continuous because:

We can always empty our cups a little to make room for new experiences and knowledge.

UNTITLED #120

While jogging, I noticed a beautiful rose blooming, basking in the gentle sunbeams. Wanting to appreciate its beauty, I naturally stopped and gazed at it with intensity, practising what is known as deep looking. The poet within me stirred, and a haiku formed in my mind:

a lovely rose blooms

with a soft touch of a sunbeam;

happiness and joy

It was then that a realisation struck me like lightning in the early morning hour. I wouldn't have enjoyed this moment had I continued running. I needed to stop and look. This idea is also supported by the famous Vietnamese monk Thich Nhat Hanh, who said that deep looking cannot be practised unless one stops running into the future and focuses on the present moment.

I believe that many of our daily problems and stresses can vanish if we learn to stop and look deeply into the present moment with a calm mind. We can experience true stillness. At that moment, I felt as if the rose was also practising that same calm and stillness.

UNTITLED #121

Command: Give what you don't want to keep.

And I started receiving promises.

UNTITLED #122

I recall the challenging years of the late 1990s and early 2000s when I would be unexpectedly overwhelmed by profound thoughts that seemed to come out of nowhere. I never questioned why, as I didn't want the flow to stop. These thoughts would enter my mind at the most inexplicable times.

One day in 1999, I once again failed to recognise a deceitful person hiding behind a mask. Due to my habit of trusting people, I felt betrayed. Sometimes it's difficult to navigate through the webs of lies and deceit, and one can become trapped. In an attempt to escape that mood, I stood outside my office on the verandah, deep in thought, when I found myself gazing at the tall coconut trees. It seemed as if they were trying to communicate something.

That's when the following words appeared in my mind, which I now share:

I always find

Trees talk to the skies and often wonder.

Do they also tell lies? Tell me, do they?

UNTITLED #123

"Thank you, sir, you truly inspire," the young person said sincerely.

"No, I live in the way I know how to. I don't do anything. Since I don't do anything, I don't inspire either," I replied with clarity.

"But sir, we feel inspired."

"That's it. It's your feeling. You feel inspired. I should be grateful to you.

Indeed, I can't inspire. It's up to you."

UNTITLED #124

I used to be a weak person, but two quotes helped me stand up and walk with my head held high.

The first quote is from Ayn Rand:

"Self-sacrifice? But it is precisely the self that cannot and must not be sacrificed." - Ayn Rand, The Fountainhead.

This made me realise that I don't always need to sacrifice my needs for others, especially since they didn't do the same for me when I needed them.

The second quote is from James Allen's "As A Man Thinketh":

"A strong man cannot help a weaker unless the weaker is willing to be helped, and even then, the weak man must become strong of himself; he must, by his own efforts, develop the strength which he admires in another. None but himself can alter his condition."

This quote taught me that I had to take responsibility for any change in myself. I courageously sought guidance and training from the right people. There is no shortcut to personal transformation.

UNTITLED #125

The other day, I went out to get a haircut. As I drove my Maruti 800 through the busy Kharadi bypass in Pune, a large car suddenly overtook me from the wrong side, quite dangerously. It seemed as if the driver had just watched one of the "Fast & Furious" movies. He was both fast and furious at me when I gestured, "Why?"

I continued driving at my leisurely pace and reached the traffic signal where I needed to turn left. There were fewer vehicles in the left-turn lane, so I was able to move forward. To my surprise, I found myself parallel to the driver who had overtaken me earlier. I glanced at him with a smile, but he looked away without returning my smile. As the light turned green, he drove straight, taking my smile with him. I didn't mind, as I knew I could quickly grow another smile in my heart. Nature and people constantly gift me seeds for smiles.

This experience made me reflect. Those we leave behind by overtaking them in life often meet us again at unexpected moments. These encounters reveal the futility of always pressing the accelerator in life. Moving ahead should also be comfortable and enjoyable! What do you think?

UNTITLED #126

"Dad, my boss asked me to do something that I'm not comfortable with. It doesn't align with my values. What should I do?"

"Just come back home and send your resignation letter. We'll figure it out."

So, the young person working in another city returned home. A couple of months passed, and his father, my friend, felt responsible for having his child leave his job. He asked me to meet with his son and try to motivate him. I agreed and met with the young man, and here's a summary of our conversation:

"Tell me, what are you feeling?" I asked.

"Uncle, I've been home for a couple of months now, and I haven't found any job opportunities. I'm starting to wonder if quitting was the right decision. I feel stuck."

I thought about it and empathised with him. However, reflecting on my own experiences, I shared a lesson I had learned:

"Sometimes, holding onto your values and stopping at a certain point is actually moving forward with greater strength. Be patient. New paths will open up. Have faith."

Soon after, he found a much better job.

UNTITLED #127

They say that sharing happiness helps us stay happy, so I'd like to share a joyful moment with you.

One evening, I was walking with my head held high when I suddenly stepped out from under cover and into the open sky. To my surprise, raindrops began to fall, creating small streams that dripped from my face. It was incredibly refreshing! I looked up and imagined the moon shining on the dark, thundering clouds, which must have appeared glorious to those above them.

At that moment, I felt connected to the rain, and my heart danced with joy. It was a beautiful experience – there was nothing between me and the sky. I felt on top of the world as if the raindrops were watery strings connecting me to my piece of the heavens. It was a magical moment that came after a lifetime of living.

That was my most precious moment up until then, and now I'm sharing it with you. By sharing this happiness, I feel even happier. Thank you!

UNTITLED #128

"Tell me about Mr X. We're considering inviting him for a session."

"Oh, Mr X? Not great. Very aggressive. He gets upset with participants if they distract him. As a trainer, he's not good."

"When did you last see him?"

"It's been a while, maybe about 5-7 years ago."

When we meet someone after many years or are asked for our opinion, we often assume that the person hasn't changed since we last met them.

On the other hand, we expect people to forget our past mistakes because we've worked on improving ourselves.

Isn't it possible that the other person has also changed? Maybe we should let go of the biases we've carried from the past. I believe we should.

UNTITLED #129

i!"

"Hi."

Silence...

"Is everything ok?"

"No, not really. I'm not in the right frame of mind."

"Do you want to talk about it?"

"No."

Both sat in silence for some time.

After about 10 minutes, neither had spoken. The one who had approached gently placed their hand on the other person's shoulder, patted it softly and left without saying a word.

They understood that sometimes people need space, and that's ok.

True happiness lies in having a friend who understands the value of their presence.

UNTITLED #130

In the Hindi movie Sultan, Aarfa sums it up perfectly in just one sentence: "We are sportsmen; we don't give up."

Now I understand what kept me going during all those years of my challenging journey. Despite being uprooted twice, I still managed to stand on my feet. I believe my sports career taught me this resilience. When you're down in a match, almost on the brink of defeat, you still choose to fight and sometimes even win. As someone once said, "It's not over until it's really over."

In fact, during a campus recruitment drive, I initiated a plan to hire at least one sportsman from each college. As it turned out, they all became go-getters and have been thriving in their respective careers.

I would advise everyone to encourage young people to pursue at least one sport during their formative years. There's no greater gift that elders can give to the younger generation.

UNTITLED #131

On Sunday, I was at Reliance Smart, as usual, buying vegetables. As I walked down an aisle with my trolley, a pomegranate rolled on the ground, having slipped from a shelf where a young girl had picked a few. I thought she would put it back, but she ignored it. I stopped, picked it up, and returned it to the shelf.

A little later, I joined another man to pick up about half a kg of okra. Despite being careful, a few pieces slipped from the tray. The man next to me and I both spontaneously bent down and picked them up, placing them back in the tray. I looked at the man and said, "Hey, thanks a lot! That was nice of you!" I then mentioned the young lady who hadn't bothered to pick up the fallen pomegranate.

He looked at me with concern and said, "It's not a big deal. It's about 'ease of life' – an unwillingness to make that extra physical effort that influences choices today."

I couldn't help but wonder if choices driven by 'ease of life' could actually help a person become strong and resilient for the challenges ahead. After all, the future won't be easy.

UNTITLED #132

Mr X, a friend, was selected for the highest award of the company in 1992 due to his outstanding all-around performance. Many people raised their eyebrows at this decision. One of them approached Mr X and asked:

"Why should you be getting the award?" "Because that's what the top management felt."

"I don't think you deserved it. So many older officers who have been performing for years deserved it more than you." Mr. X replied, "I don't know. Maybe it was a mistake! Is that possible?" The man didn't react, so Mr X continued, "Ok, let's see how it must have happened.

1st mistake - My boss recommended me. 2nd - His boss forwarded it to the VP.

3rd - The VP endorsed it for the committee's review. 4th - The MD put the final proposal to the Chairman.

Finally, maybe it was the Chairman who would be signing my certificate. I think I should go to the Chairman and tell him about your concern and ask him not to consider me. Should I? Why carry the burden of their mistake and become a target of people like you?"

The man had a strange, frightened look on his face and left in a hurry.

UNTITLED #133

"You don't know what I can do," the boss said, staring at him. Instilling fear in people's minds was his way of running the show.

The subordinate looked at him, smiled, and said, "You think you are powerful, don't you? Here's your 'power' over me, going with the wind out there from that window. Look..."

He took a folded paper out of his pocket and placed it in front of the boss. It was his resignation letter.

The illusion of power shattered.

Power in the corporate world is so fragile.

The wise ones understand this. That's why they never wield power. Instead, they help people around them feel empowered. They help their colleagues become fearless. They create an environment of learning, growth, and development. They are humble yet firm when necessary.

UNTITLED #134

He appeared educated and quite sophisticated, smoking a cigarette right at the entrance of a restaurant. I needed space to enter, and the air had a thin layer of smoke. I politely asked him to move a little farther from the entrance to avoid discomfort. He looked at me with very hostile eyes and didn't move. I proceeded inside.

II

He didn't appear well groomed, rough and tough, someone you'd prefer to keep at arm's length. He was sitting on a step right at the entrance of the shop where I visit daily to buy regular packets of Amul Tazza Milk. Despite not being sure of the outcome, as the earlier incident lingered in my mind, I asked him to move a little away so that those coming to the shop at that early hour could breathe better air. He said, "Sorry, sir," and got up to move to a safer distance. His eyes didn't show any hostility, his face remained calm, and he was comfortable with my request.

Once again, the saying that looks can be deceptive proved to be true.

UNTITLED #135

There were some dreams that clung to me, even though I knew they could never be fulfilled, things which were beyond my reach. So, I found an interesting way to let them go.

I closed my eyes, gathered them, and placed them in a small paper boat. Then, I gently released the boat into the streams formed by my tears. I watched it sail away, and due to the weight, the boat slowly sank, taking my dreams with it. Within moments, my dreams dissolved and became water.

The water continued to flow, and new dreams arrived with the current. These were happier, more peaceful dreams—the kind that, if pursued, would lead me to the place I always longed to be. I chose a few of them, let them enter my heart, and savoured them. Now, after almost three decades, I see them slowly manifesting. This book is among those dreams.

UNTITLED #136

"Good morning!" I said.

"What's so good about the morning, huh?" he asked with a rather repulsive expression.

Looking at him, I replied, "You! You're what's good about this morning."

His expression changed. The repulsive look turned into one of surprise, and then his face slowly relaxed.

I could see the morning smile, just like the yellow flowers in the flower bed that seemed to be smiling too. Had they heard what I said to him? I wonder.

UNTITLED #137

Learning, constantly learning, and sharing was my destiny.

At that time, I couldn't understand. But then, God worked through many people, making them show their worst to take away my smile, which was more the product of external stimuli.

God wanted to ensure that I had no other choice but to learn to grow the smile in my heart whenever I felt like it. And I learned because that was God's plan for me. I learned it well.

Now, I can not only grow more smiles but also have plenty to share with you all. Here's tossing a bunch of them through these words. Let me know if you can catch one. Ha, ha, I can see that clean catch. You know what's so wonderful about it? You've already grown a beautiful smile and thrown it back at me to catch.

I know it's going to rain today. And I'll see a rainbow of smiles forming in the skies of my inner space.

UNTITLED #138

Some people find it hard to believe when I say - I am a very happy person. I practice happiness all the time. They question how I can claim to be happy when:

- I don't yet have a proper, bigger house to settle down in.
- I don't work regularly like many others, with far less experience in the same profession.
- I still have some major domestic responsibilities to fulfil.

Indeed, it makes me wonder too. How can I be happy when what they say is part of my reality?

But then I check my feelings. I still feel happier, much happier! That's because I focus on what I have:

- I have a small house that would be enough to accommodate me and my spouse if ever needed.
- I occasionally get work from people who trust me for who and what I am, and more keeps getting added to the list.
- I have a few loving family members who support me, making my responsibilities much less intimidating.
- I have God by my side, who helps me in His own miraculous ways.

UNTITLED #139

"Do you remember, sir, the other day I called you up and told you that it pained me so much that despite working for so many years in a department, I wasn't even offered a farewell party?" he asked me.

"Yes, I remember. So, what is it about?" I asked.

"Sir, you told me to shift my thought and re-frame it. So, I re-framed it, sir, and I have gotten rid of my pain."

"Ok, tell me how it happened?"

"Well, I just created a scene of my farewell happening to see what I would see, hear, or feel, as suggested by you, and found that those who were responsible for finding ways and excuses to finally ensure that it never happened were also all praise for me. Everyone was applauding my efforts and sharing how much I would be missed."

"Is that so? Did you like it?"

"No, sir, that's more painful. They weren't telling the truth. They hated me for my achievements and ensured that it never happened. I am feeling much better now that it didn't happen."

UNTITLED #140

I asked a friend about the types of assignments that had been most satisfying for him and contributed to his successful career. I wanted to learn about the common features of those assignments.

He shared the following commonalities:

- They were very challenging assignments and not everyone's cup of tea.
- They primarily involved resolving issues to make stuck things move, which required a lot of creative thinking.
- He had the freedom to do them his way, including planning his own strategy.
- He was trusted for the outcome.
- The outcome always succeeded in generating envy, telling him that he had truly done well.

Every point resonated with me, and I asked him if I could add:

- The credit for those assignments often got shared with others who hadn't contributed even a bit to achieving those outcomes.

He agreed.

UNTITLED #141

A LinkedIn connection and HR Professional were leaving the city and had called me for a chat. When we were together, he said, "RS Sir, today I'll be leaving Pune and thought I must meet you once before I leave. I have been reading your posts and would like to spend some moments exchanging thoughts with you. Can we have lunch together?" It was an honour. We met at a nearby restaurant.

During our conversation, we drifted towards the topic of "unsolicited advice" that we tend to give to people. I mentioned that we should never do that. Despite its roots in good intentions, unsolicited advice often becomes one of the biggest reasons for discord, even in families.

Prashant listened and candidly said, "Sir, sometimes one has to take that risk. It doesn't matter." After a pause, he continued, "I remember advising a young executive to do a certain assignment in a particular way to get the desired outcome. However, he didn't agree and said that he had his own style. But there are certain standard ways of doing things that experience knows. You can't put shoes on first and socks over them and then say this is my style. No, sometimes we must do things our own way."

Indeed, I agreed with him.

UNTITLED #142

You are sitting with friends, and you do something interesting that you've learned over time because you have a talent for it. You find someone telling you, "So what! It isn't difficult. I can do it too." That's when you need to ask the person to demonstrate it. Obviously, they wouldn't do it because they can't. You've practised it. You've learned it. They haven't. Yet, the ego doesn't want to accept your effort and that you are better.

Nothing can replace constant focused practice to justify your talent. Merely having talent and then doing nothing to develop it further would often lead to missing out on the opportunity to come face to face with the purpose of your life.

So, here are just three steps:

Identify your talent.

Identify who can help you develop it further.

Practice under the guidance of a master.

While I don't have any regrets, if I had known earlier in my life that my talent for writing poetry meant my ability to observe human behaviour deeply, I would have accomplished some milestones earlier.

UNTITLED #143

After hearing his story about becoming a victim of lies and deceit from his own, he spoke those familiar golden words, "One day their soul will shake them up, and they will realise. I trust God." I had heard these words many times before and even spoken them myself.

I asked him plainly, "What if it doesn't happen and they don't realise?" He was quiet, then asked, "Why should you say that?" I responded, "It's possible, isn't it?" I said this because it hadn't happened, and they hadn't realised. He thought it over and asked, "Then what should I do?"

Drawing from my own experience, I advised, "Learn from this moment. It's good to be trustworthy, but be careful and assess before trusting others. Now that you've already been hurt, you can't let it happen again. Burning your fingers twice can get you stuck. You need your fingers to push the buttons in elevators that take you up. Ha, ha... Isn't that right?"

He understood the joke and thanked me with a smile, which I collected like so many others. I need them because they work like seeds to grow more.

I also understood the reason for my own difficult experiences. I was meant to share and help people handle their wounds with care and confidence, allowing for better and faster healing.

UNTITLED #144

Want to enjoy your day without letting any negative vibes affect it?

Simply stand up, look at the sky, and say out loud - "I have decided to be happy throughout the day. Nothing will make me lose my balance."

Stay still, smile, and let the words resonate in your mind for a few moments. I promise, they will remind you of your decision during times when you might feel tempted to be uncomfortable.

Just make the decision - and why wouldn't you?

UNTITLED #145

I met him at the bookstore, an acquaintance from a professional group. We started a small conversation about a few books when he changed the subject and said:

"You know, after you left the other day, we were discussing how the evening went. This gentleman made a subtle statement in the group that put you down. Without your knowledge, your credibility among the young minds must have been affected. Your presentation lost some impact. He created doubts and left before anyone could question him." The man seemed genuinely concerned.

He was referring to a demonstration I had given to a group about a week earlier. I simply smiled and asked him politely, "Why would you tell me this?"

He looked astonished and struggled to understand, then said, "You need to know what people say about you behind your back."

I asked, "How does it help you?"

He wasn't prepared for the answer, so he didn't respond. Everyone's words and actions have a positive intention from their perspective. I just wanted to know one thing: How could speaking negatively about someone in their absence be positive for anyone? Think about it.

UNTITLED #146

"Sir, I have a question for you," a young fellow professional asked me as we sipped coconut water through thin straws. Sometimes, standing under a tree holding coconuts and having discussions is more satisfying than sitting and chatting in an air-conditioned café or a 5-star hotel.

"Go ahead."

"I've seen many professionals enthusiastically exchanging business cards. But when one tries to connect with them, they ignore the call. A WhatsApp message shows those green ticks giving hope, yet fails to get a reply. SMS faces the same fate. Why do people exchange business cards if they don't want others to connect with them?"

"Well, the 'why' can be answered only by them. I can share what I think. Is that OK?"

"Yes sir, please tell me."

"Let's understand one thing. Your number is not saved in their phone. So when you call, it's an unknown number to them, and they might ignore it if they're busy. A better way is to send them an SMS giving reference to your meeting and asking for a suitable time to talk."

"Sir, if they don't respond to that, then what?"

"Then it's even more clear that they don't want you to bother them. Take the hint and relax."

UNTITLED #147

Every transaction, regardless of its nature, ultimately involves two people. If they choose to make the transaction successful without focusing on their individual success and self-interest, the business world would be a much better place.

Many businesses fail prematurely because people focus on a single need:

"I must get more than you."

UNTITLED #148

I was snubbed, snubbed badly on every page of presentation that I had thought was my best work till date. The Boss was able to find something to criticize on every page. It had never happened with me and none had expected it to happen. Did anyone come to my rescue?

My question to you is this: Does anyone ever?' Well, I was taken aback for a minute. And then the darkness withered away. It was all light and I prepared myself for some more hits till the end.

No, it wasn't that the presentation was bad. It was bad mood of the Boss that made him behave like that. He was compelled by his own inner environment.

I had only made a valiant attempt earlier evening to defend someone who was absent from the attack by another closer to the power. So, the Power was given the feedback. I am sure before coming to the meeting room he must have told himself, "I will show him. How dare he?' And well , the interaction turned out to be amazingly life-transforming.

UNTITLED #149

"Sir, I am very happy."

"Why?"

"I won a strong argument. It took almost an hour!"

"What was the argument about?"

"Sir, it was about cricket administration."

"How does that concern you?"

"It does, sir. I love cricket. I proved my point."

"And will anything change because you won the argument with an acquaintance after spending so much time?"

"No, but it feels good, sir. A small success for me!"

I couldn't bring myself to congratulate him. I was concerned that his need to find joy and feel good in such small victories would consume a lot of his time in life without adding any value to him or anyone else.

Looking back, I see many red dots on the timeline of my life. Those red dots represented moments or hours when I had spent time winning small battles that lacked any meaningful purpose. Experiencing joy after such victories or meaningless successes can be addictive, counterproductive, and ultimately futile in the long run.

UNTITLED #150

I have always enjoyed whistling old Bollywood songs. I recall an incident from around 1995-1996 when my son was about 9-10 years old.

One fine Thursday morning (in the place where I lived, Thursday was like Sunday for others), I was sitting idle in my room when I suddenly heard my son trying to whistle. My wife, from the kitchen, almost shouted, "No, son, whistling is not good."

My son replied, "But Papa also whistles."

My wife said, "But Papa is Papa..."

Quickly, my son responded, "And a whistle is a whistle. If it's bad for me, it's bad for him."

This was the first life lesson that greatly helped me in my profession and training. I learned the importance of leading by example. One cannot rely on good talk alone without applying it to one's own life. This lesson has served me well ever since.

UNTITLED #151

A friend wanted to know some tips about public speaking.

I recalled my first experience speaking to a group of engineering students back in 1994-95. The session began with around 70 attendees, and I was warned that it might dwindle to just 30-35 by the end. However, I had never spoken publicly before, and by the time I finished my talk, the hall was packed with over 150 students.

What did I do?

I spoke their language – a mix of English, Hindi, and Marathi – and discussed a topic that was relevant to their needs, which is now referred to as "campus to corporate." I was candid and open about real-life situations. I used humour that they could relate to, which made them laugh along with me. I answered every question confidently, satisfying their curiosity. I kept it simple by using everyday examples from a corporate setting. My talk was original, and they hadn't heard anything like it before.

Throughout my speech, I maintained a cheerful demeanour and smiled, showing that I was genuinely happy to be among them. My happiness was evident on my face, and it contributed to the success of my first public speaking experience.

UNTITLED #152

I encountered him looking quite sad. He had been a participant in one of my training sessions, and we happened to run into each other at a bookstore. After some casual conversation, I asked,

"What's wrong? You seem upset."

"Sir, I lost two friends."

"Oh, how did that happen?"

"Well, one was a childhood friend. He had a heart attack, and stress took his life. The other was a colleague who betrayed me. I had taken on a challenge with my management for a project, relying on his promise of total help and support. However, he went against the project during a meeting. I was deeply embarrassed and lost face. It came as a shock to me."

Losing one friend to death and another to betrayal had the same impact on him. I could completely relate to his situation.

This highlights one of the fascinating aspects of the corporate world. Affinities can shift rapidly as dynamics change. One must always remain cautious and careful.

UNTITLED #153

In 1982, I landed my first and only job. To celebrate, I bought a new Bajaj Scooter and rode it to the office. When my superior found out, he congratulated me, asked for the keys, and kick-started my scooter. He then made me sit behind him and took me for a ride. Was I happy? Absolutely!

This gesture showed how true leaders view their team members as extended family, sharing in their moments of joy.

Throughout their careers, genuine leaders maintain consistent behaviour. While their responsibilities may change, their core values remain the same.

UNTITLED #154

Certain events that boost one's confidence remain etched in our memories. For me, it was in 2011.

I remember visiting a wellness club for a few days after leaving my job. During my time there, I met a couple of school teachers and shared my experiences with them. After about three days, one of them called and asked if I would conduct a 90-minute session for parents of 11th and 12th-grade students on managing and reducing stress at home to help their children perform better. I agreed, and around 100 parents attended the session. I hoped that they would implement the advice I shared. That was my first-ever session in Pune.

Almost a year later, my wife and I visited an optician to buy glasses for her. After making our purchase, we waited outside for an auto-rickshaw. Suddenly, the shop owner approached us and asked, "Aren't you Mr Ramesh Sood?" Surprised, I replied, "Yes, I am." She continued, "I wanted to thank you for the session at the school last year. I couldn't do so that day, as you left immediately and I was sitting in the last row. Your advice helped us and our child. I wasn't sure, but your voice seemed familiar. We are grateful."

That day, my wife realised that I was on the right path.

UNTITLED #155

During a morning walk, I notice a pink and a red rose swaying in the breeze, their attention captured by the fluttering wings of a nearby butterfly. Miraculously, I can hear the thoughts and conversations between the flowers and the butterfly. I hear the red rose exclaim,

"Hey, come here, here!"

The butterfly smiles, responding with a twinkle, "Yes, that's what I cherish most - my freedom of choice within the confines of God's wish. Let me wait for the signal."

As she hums a hopeful tune, a sunbeam illuminates her colourful wings. She leaps onto it and gently descends into the embrace of the blooming pink rose.

The pink rose is overjoyed with the gift, while the hopeful red rose feels envious, silently cursing their happiness. The butterfly notices the red rose's feelings and silently admires him, thinking,

"Maybe tomorrow morning," as she prays for him.

Both the butterfly and the red rose exercise their freedom of thought in these moments based on their own evolution in nature's embrace. May the butterfly's prayer lead her to the red rose, transforming his thoughts. The beautiful world of happier thoughts deserves to expand, and indeed, it does!

UNTITLED #156

"Sir, I want to quickly learn how to build a successful career. Can you give me a short course in about 15 minutes?"

This request was challenging, but I accepted it. I asked him, "Tell me the best way to destroy your own career in a company."

He thought for a moment and responded, "I think it's easy. Just do three things: one, always brag about yourself and make your colleagues feel inferior at every opportunity; two, be alert to find their faults and criticise them openly, showing that you can always do better; and three, always talk against your boss behind their back. If anyone does these three things regularly, they'll hasten their exit."

He made sense, and I smiled. He then asked, "But what should I do to grow, be liked, and build my career?"

I replied, "By doing the exact opposite of what you just told me. Simple. So, tell me what that would be?"

He thought and said, "The opposite? Okay. Be humble; let others feel good in your presence; always find reasons to appreciate them, and never talk badly about your boss, even if asked by a higher-up. Continue to update your knowledge."

My session was over in less than 15 minutes.

UNTITLED #157

Shortest Course on Leadership

"Why are you here?" I asked.

"Sir, to become leaders," they replied.

"Why?"

"Because we want to lead."

"Have you ever followed?" I questioned.

"No, sir!"

"Then you must follow first."

"Whom do we follow, sir? There are no leaders in our vicinity, only bosses."

"Can you follow your own principles and values strictly under all circumstances?"

"Yes, sir," they answered.

"Then first, follow them to lead yourself. You will learn all about becoming a leader."

They agreed to first identify their values to lead their own lives - a crucial first step towards leadership. The rest is all in the details.

UNTITLED #158

My part in the meeting had concluded, and as I prepared to leave, the chair asked me to stay and contribute to the discussion on the Vision Statement, Objectives, and Values. The top management group seemed to recognise my ability to think conceptually and creatively. I felt honoured, even though I was lower in the hierarchy.

During the presentation, I found myself uncomfortable with a couple of lines that had already been proposed and agreed upon. Despite my instincts telling me to hold back, I couldn't resist sharing my thoughts during a pause. The senior executives looked at me with expressionless faces, and one of them overruled my suggestion, leaving it unchanged.

A few moments later, the young Managing Director, who had briefly left the room, returned and instructed that my suggestion be implemented. No one could object, and the change was made.

True leaders don't let their egos interfere and always prioritise the content of the message rather than the person delivering it.

UNTITLED #159

I recently encountered an acquaintance who praised my thoughts and writing, promising to help me with my work. He mentioned that he had great respect for me.

A few days later, I spotted him in a mall, walking towards me with two other people. I waited to greet him. As he approached, he completely ignored me, turning his face away. If he had just glanced my way, I would have acknowledged him with a nod. He didn't, and he never called back, either.

My concern for him is this:

If you choose to be a two-faced person, you may eventually reach a point where no one, including yourself, can recognise your true face—the one you were born with and meant to carry throughout your life.

UNTITLED #160

I understand your health concerns. You're just one decision away from improving your well-being. If you haven't already, simply choose to take long walks every morning or evening, according to your schedule and comfort level.

By doing so, you'll experience a life-changing boost in positive energy. Every aspect of your life will improve, without a doubt. If you're already walking regularly, consider focusing on rhythmic breathing to enhance the experience. It's truly magical.

Let me be clear: any health discussion should include the importance of morning or evening walks.

The most significant benefit of walking is gaining freedom from the monsters called stress and depression. So, as you go to bed tonight, decide to go for a walk. It's all about making that decision.

Get up, get set, and go!

UNTITLED #161

I recently killed a cockroach, which, like all creatures, was trying its best to survive. However, for the sake of my own survival and to protect a young child who used the room as a play area, I had to act against it. This response was instinctive, as nature expects us to protect ourselves and our loved ones.

This experience led me to consider that, as part of nature, some people—much more powerful than me—have also been unfair to me. They did so not only to survive but to grow, acting as they knew best. The only difference is that the cockroach had already entered my territory, while those people acted against me preemptively, fearing I might encroach on theirs.

In hindsight, I should have been sharper, smarter, and stronger to protect myself. At the time, I was as vulnerable as that cockroach. I've come to understand that we attract circumstances based on our own strengths and weaknesses. Therefore, we should continuously strive to become stronger.

The world may be unfair at times, but that's okay. We'll face challenges effectively by embracing our growth and resilience.

UNTITLED #162

I recall attending a brief session led by a senior executive over two decades ago. During the session, he posed an interesting question: "When we interview people, they confidently share how their strengths will benefit the company and commit to giving their best. But after settling in, they often exhibit behaviors stemming from their weaknesses more than their strengths. Why does this happen?"

Years later, a billiards match provided me with an answer.

In the semi-final match, I noticed the score with just six minutes remaining. I had a comfortable lead and thought I should play it safe to secure the win. Instead of scoring, I focused on playing defensively and ended up losing. This is similar to what happens in the corporate world. We often concentrate on keeping threats at bay, which divides our energy. Our basic instinct is to protect ourselves, and this drive.

UNTITLED #163

"Why are you looking upset?" I asked.

"Sir, my brother was rude to me this morning."

"Is he always rude?"

"No, sir."

"Frequently?"

"No, sir."

"Then...?"

"Sometimes; it hurts, you know."

"Well, listen carefully. It's challenging for humans to be consistently good and polite. Have you always been kind and courteous to him?"

He looked surprised and didn't respond, so I continued:

"Sometimes, we lose balance, and that's okay. If he wasn't in the right frame of mind today, stay calm. You might not be the reason. Just sit quietly and have a cup of tea together. It's okay to be upset occasionally."

"What about you, sir?"

"Even if I'm usually good, I can't be that way all the time. I also act irrationally sometimes. But I bounce back and don't dwell on it for more than a few minutes."

He pondered and said, "And here I am, carrying it for the last 480 minutes." "Don't," I advised. He laughed.

UNTITLED #164

I recall those times when I would meditate on the rising sun in a beautiful garden. Ah, those moments of meditation when I needed nothing; when I noticed nothing; when I just wouldn't be my body; when I would just BE ; when I would become a living prayer; flowing with the music of my own breath; ah sheer bliss that!

I loved being in that state of happiness when somewhere work waited for me; when an opportunity to justify my own existence would beckon me; when I would be making that subtle positive difference in the lives of some people without even being aware of that; when I would face storms without realising those were storms; when I would just be in the moment to do what the moment expected; when under some uncontrollable moments I would get happily angry, happily sad, happily upset, happily tearful, happily hurt and be back joyously happy. It feels good that I am back joyously happy and have started reliving some moments like that.

Let me invite you to do this: Just be a soul for some moments in the day that dances to the music of its own pure breath, knowing that the rest doesn't matter and let life flow in those moments, just for a few moments flow, without judging anything, in total acceptance.

I see God smiling. I am happy. Aren't you too?

UNTITLED #165

Heartbreak happens, and we often assign blame. Instead of pointing fingers, it's better to use those fingers to gather the pieces, mend them carefully, and watch a stronger heart emerge swiftly.

However, don't hesitate to pick up the pieces, as the winds of passing moments may sweep away small, fragile ones. You might find some crucial pieces missing.

You may wonder how I can say this with confidence. Well, experience matters, doesn't it?

And remember, hearts can break for countless reasons, not just romantic relationships.

Take care.

UNTITLED #166

In 1989, as a Purchase Coordinator, I was sent to Mumbai to obtain a few steel bars of a specific grade from a regular supplier. The task was challenging since we hadn't paid the supplier on time for previous supplies due to financial difficulties, and he was reluctant. I wasn't sure how he would react, but I had to take the chance. When I arrived at his office, he refused to entertain me as I stood at his door. He glared at me and began expressing his anger. I had a deliberate inability to hear when someone shouted since words never made sense in such a state.

As he was shouting, my eyes wandered around his cabin, which seemed to be an architectural wonder. Eventually, he grew tired. Without any conscious thought, I smiled and said, "I understand, sir. I won't talk business. But let me come in and discuss your beautifully designed office. Who is the architect?" He gave me an astonished look, paused, let me in, and said, "I did it myself." For the next half an hour, we discussed architecture, and I introduced him to the book "The Fountainhead" by Ayn Rand.

What do you think happened regarding the material?

UNTITLED #167

She was talking to her husband about her colleague and said, "Mrs XYZ really seems to think too highly of herself. You know, she meets me every morning during our walks. She never even says hello and just walks by."

Her husband smiled and said, "It happens when both people are similar."

She was upset, "How can you say that? I'm not like her."

The man replied, "No, just look at it this way. She must be having a similar conversation about you with her husband, right? Think about it."

Now, I don't know if she thought about it. But we need to. It's so easy to say 'hello' first to anyone, isn't it? Often, we criticise people for not doing things that we ourselves don't do.

UNTITLED #168

"RS, I understand you'll be busier in the coming days. So, are we likely to miss your updates and the stories we read every day?" he asked me quite frankly.

"No, why would you think that? Anyone on this planet can find time to do what they're passionate about. I will too" I replied spontaneously.

What do you think? Am I right? Time management only comes into play when we're doing things that we consider compulsory and require conscious effort, doesn't it? Passion finds its moments to indulge.

UNTITLED #169

"You're incredibly, absolutely, extremely, supremely, unbelievably different." – Kami Garcia.

I wholeheartedly agree with Kami Garcia. My only note of caution is this:

Don't tell anyone that you are different. Just be with people without any pressing need to show it. Gradually, they will start noticing that special glow on your face and the gleam in your eyes. They will begin talking about it. Let them. You may even start receiving special treatment. Take it in stride. When you first hear someone speaking enviously, that's the time to give yourself a pat on the back. You know then that you have arrived. That's when you can demonstrate to the world your uniqueness by staying calm and praying for the evolution of those souls.

UNTITLED #170

"RS, yesterday some people were talking quite humorously about you."

"If you meet them, please say thanks on my behalf."

"Thanks? You should confront them."

"Why? Can there be a better compliment than people spending some portion of their precious life thinking and talking about me, rather than focusing on themselves?" He gave me a puzzled look.

I can only hope that after contemplating it, he understood. It doesn't matter; have you grasped the concept?

UNTITLED #171

"I am MAGICAL."

Hey, this isn't about me. I want you to say it to yourself and decide to create magic with your words or your work, NOW. Please don't worry about your age or think that I'm asking you to be childish. Yes, I am. So what? Being and behaving childlike brings pure joy.

Magic can't be in the past or the future. It must be created NOW. Are you missing it? Really? Then stop reading. Stand up and do or say something that will create magic. It could be just a cheerful HELLO to yourself or those around you, and trust me, the smiles that will appear on those faces will be magical.

Ah, writing this here is so magical for me! Yes, it is!

Let's practice our freedom to choose JOY and happiness every day... That will be a true celebration.

UNTITLED #172

I engage in regular self-talks every day. Oh, what a revelation I had today during one such conversation between I & Me!

The great thing about self-talk is that you can reprimand yourself, tear yourself apart, and be utterly ruthless, all without anyone else knowing. The pain you experience often leads you to the right path.

The greater truth is that when the mind becomes familiar with this pain, it does everything it can to help you make happier choices and fewer mistakes. Eventually, it leads you to a state where every corner of your inner space is illuminated. If there's a corner you can't reach that remains somewhat dark, you know that a thin, shining beam of awareness must be touching it too.

Self-talk. A very sincere and honest self-talk is the most powerful tool for self-change.

UNTITLED #173

Once upon a time, a long time ago, when I was a young man of about 19, I met a very senior fellow on a deluxe train while travelling from Ludhiana to New Delhi. We were sitting next to each other. I had asked him how one could stay happy in life. He had given me a beautiful answer, which went something like this:

"As long as your body is functioning well at its optimum capacity and you know what you're going to do during the day to set up a happier tomorrow, you have no reason to be unhappy. If you still manage to find a reason, then you've brought it from outside yourself. So stay focused on yourself, and stay healthy, fresh, and alive. Do what needs to be done, and if time permits, do what you want to do."

I listened carefully to his words, and they have guided me throughout my journey. I am focused on 'Needs' more than 'Wants.' It's essential to make a clear distinction. For example, we need to stay healthy. We cannot 'want' to stay healthy. We need to give our best to work and cannot 'want' to give our best.

You WANT to remember this. No, you NEED to remember this.

UNTITLED #174

He was asked by his boss to resign after spending countless years working honestly.

Visibly upset, he stood in front of his boss and said, "I will never forgive you."

The boss didn't react or respond. They usually don't. He left, deeply angered.

When we met a couple of years after that event, he shared the moment with me.

I asked him, "So, to keep your word, what did you do NOT TO FORGIVE HIM?"

He appeared puzzled. I repeated the question. He said, "What could I do, RS? I never saw his face again."

"By not seeing his face ever again, how did it affect him?"

He thought for a minute and couldn't answer.

"It means nothing happened to him. He has been enjoying a good career and even having fun harassing you in your thoughts without even knowing it. Right?"

I wanted him to think. "Yes, you are right, RS."

"It's not about forgiving him. It's about moving forward and not remaining stuck there."

I told him how to consciously dilute the memory. It's all about conscious awareness and practice.

The last I heard of him, he was enjoying his freedom.

UNTITLED #175

As we discussed his career, he said, "RS, it started when my super-boss called me and said, 'See, I am very impressed with the way you think and draft letters & notes. Our friend, Mr. X, has prepared a note to be sent to the MD. Somehow he is not able to express himself well and use the right words. I want you to correct it and then give it back to him.' My super-boss took my agreement for granted and dismissed us both.

"Along with my own work, I spent a couple of hours rewriting the note for my colleague, who then signed it and received all the accolades. This became a ritual. First, it was notes, then PPTs got added, not only for him but for all the other functions and their managers who reported to the same super-boss. I would sit late nights to do my work. Life got extremely busy. No time for family. I was being used and denied rewards and any credit for that. No one noticed. I was getting completely drained. It took me years to make a decision. RS, write about this. Tell people that the day they feel their talent is being exploited, they must make a choice and move away."

He wanted me to share his story, so I have.

UNTITLED #176

"My friend seemed upset as he said, "I really feel jealous of him for the kind of contacts he has."

"You feel jealous? Is that it?" I wanted to be sure.

"Yes, RS, I do," he confirmed.

"How do you feel jealous? I mean, what do you do or show that would let me know you're feeling jealous of someone?" I asked, genuinely curious.

He appeared a bit flustered as he asked, "What do you mean, RS?"

"Exactly what I asked. I mean, you must be doing something inside or outside of you to feel jealous, right?" I spoke.

He looked confused. Then he said, "I don't know. Maybe something inside changes. I mean, one gets a bit angry or upset when seeing the person they're jealous of. There could be some stiffness in the facial muscles or a bad feeling in the stomach, RS, or some movement of my eyes; something happens."

"Well, try to understand it. Recognise it and then work on calming those muscles or keeping your eyes still. It can be done by actually becoming aware of the emotion. It dilutes," I shared the trick with him.

And then, as an afterthought, I said, "And work on yourself to become worthy of the attention of those whom you give undue attention."

UNTITLED #177

"Can a person practice happiness without practicing it at home?"

"No, that's not possible."

"So, what is your secret?"

"Simple, keeping it all simple. Everyone has the right to be upset, but not for more than a couple of minutes because life is slipping away at the rate of 60 minutes per hour. Isn't it?"

"Oh, that's nice."

"And one more thing. Whoever finishes their exercise or morning walk earlier, either my spouse or I make the morning tea for both of us. No set rules. Try it. It helps a lot."

UNTITLED #178

"No, I mean it's very difficult to stay together. He just doesn't understand me."

"Then, it's easy. It's in your hands."

"How?"

"Understand him," I was clear in my advice.

She looked at me with a stunned expression. And then, after a few moments, her facial muscles relaxed.

We spent the next few minutes in silence.

I could suddenly sense comfort in her voice as she said, "Yes, it makes sense. I didn't know it was so easy."

"It is. We just need to shift our perspective. We just need to take that one step outside of ourselves."

There were a few moments of silence. Then she said, "Thanks a lot, RS. It helps."

And with that, since there wasn't much left to discuss on the subject, we enjoyed our coffee in silence with some soothing music playing in the background.

Indeed, the breeze of understanding can be so refreshing to our senses. Life becomes beautiful.

UNTITLED #179

Once, I was asked, "RS, does 'professionalism' allow professionals to make promises they don't intend to keep, just to get through moments of intense emotional compulsions or pressures?"

My answer:

No, nothing justifies a gesture like this because the person who makes a promise has given hope to another, who will now wait for the 'promise' to become a reality and feel disappointed when it doesn't. They will feel even worse when they learn the truth and, worst of all, when they discover that this is the norm and lose faith in professionals.

Therefore, real professionals, even if they are under similar circumstances, will never make a promise they don't intend to keep. Such individuals make the world a more beautiful place.

UNTITLED #180

For about four years, he was waiting for his school bus with his mum as I was walking past them in the morning. The boy looked at me and spontaneously said,

"I know you. You are my dad's opponent in TT." Surprised, I said, "No, not opponent. Your dad is my TT friend. We play together."

He was clear, "The one who plays from the other side is an opponent." I was speechless.

Wow, clarity with spontaneity, two traits of childhood. I was wondering as I walked - Where do we leave them? Why don't we continue to keep them with us forever?

That's when I looked up. The sun had just come up in the east. Its rays hitting my face whispered some words in my ears. I got my answer. Yes, the afternoon sun will never be able to reflect the innocence of the rising sun, that glorious golden quiet glow, and the evening sun won't have the strength of the afternoon sun. That's how nature works. I was also part of nature. It was alright if doubt had replaced clarity and careful consideration had replaced spontaneity in the afternoon of my life. And it was alright to gain clarity about things with conscious effort. Growing older also means accepting some essential changes in our behaviours.

UNTITLED #181

As the discussion progressed and became more intense, he suddenly revealed something very personal, a kind of secret. I was surprised and asked, "Why should you share this?"

He was very candid and clear,

"Sir, sharing it with you, I feel unburdened." I was slightly uncomfortable and said,

"But how can you trust me?"

He replied, "Sir, I choose to trust you." I still wanted to make him aware,

"If I betray you, then?"

He looked at me with great intensity and said, "That will be your choice."

In those moments, I realised that there is no bigger compliment than someone telling you -

"I trust you."

I learned to choose trust.

We can choose to become trustworthy to let life smile more.

UNTITLED #182

Here's to happiness!

You've probably spent at least half an hour throughout the day cursing or criticising someone else.

Now, do yourself and me a favour. Just sit and think positively about yourself for five minutes.

Do this every day. Then, experience the magic after a few days. You'll fall in love with yourself.

All the best!

UNTITLED #183

Many people have asked me why I was never in a hurry to do things. Yes, I have noticed this too.

I believe that what gets registered in our minds after we contemplate certain sayings during intense moments often gives birth to new beliefs. This is perhaps what happened. A couple of quotes made me stop and think, and yes, repetition in my mind transformed me from someone who is always in a hurry to a person who prefers to be in the flow, always doing what needs to be done at a comfortable speed.

Let me share two of those sayings here. The first quote I loved during those days, which I had then put in my cabin when I was working for a corporate, read:

"Nature does not hurry. Yet everything gets accomplished."

Lao Tzu

The learning was reinforced when I read this behind a truck on the highway: "Jinhe Zaldi thii, woh chale gaye." (Those who were in a hurry went.)

It has helped me, and stress has become somewhat of a stranger.

UNTITLED #184

"RS Sir, what does it take to start a business?"

I've always felt hesitant to answer this question because I haven't been able to consider it for myself, despite many people encouraging me to start a School of Day-to-Day Happiness.

Naturally, the answer would involve doing the things I haven't been able to do. Three of those are:

I don't consider myself to have reached or arrived anywhere. So, to start a business, one needs the confidence to become a brand and grow.

I don't have a solid backup for resources, having started from zero and worked for someone else for a long time. I lack the ability to take risks. So, one will need the ability to take risks with an appropriate solid backup.

I'm incapable of saying 'Yes' when I want to say 'No'. So, one will have to learn to say 'Yes' on some occasions despite reluctance. One will need to learn to make uncomfortable decisions.

As for now, my answer is 'No' for myself. But you, go for it.

UNTITLED #185

"RS, I feel like I'm a very negative person. I want to become more positive."

"How do you know you're negative?"

"I always focus on finding faults in people and things."

"Then we need to use your ability to focus more on finding the good in others. I'm sure you also think positively on occasions."

"Yes, RS, there are times when I am positive."

"And your conversation with me today about what you perceive as wrong in yourself, with the goal of improving, is itself a very positive action. So change your statement to - RS, I want to expand my focus on the positive a bit more than the negative, which currently takes a lot of energy - say it." And she did.

Then she smiled and said, "RS, I feel better. I think I was influenced by the people around me and what they said about me."

"Remember, you are a positive person. You only attempt to correct mistakes in people. Sometimes it's the words you use to express yourself that seem negative. So if you feel compelled to say something, just change the words."

She understood as I wrapped up one of my shortest sessions on Developing a Positive Attitude.

UNTITLED #186

A few years ago, a little boy grabbed the lower edge of my jacket as I walked towards the main entrance of a shopping mall, asking for alms. I refused. As he persisted, I nearly shouted at him, saying, "I don't have any money, please. OK, now leave me."

He looked at me and said, "What, sir? You're going to such a big, expensive mall, and you're telling me you don't have money, huh?!"

His reaction amazed me. I paused and chose to ignore him.

Looking back, I realise that he had used a verbal trick that people have been using for centuries. They want you to help them by provoking a feeling of guilt in you for being in a better position. It takes awareness and a pause not to fall into such an emotional trap.

Be careful! There could be people wearing masks, playing with your emotion day in and day out, and seeking your support or help.

UNTITLED #187

Sometime in 2018, I experienced some truly anxious moments as I traveled at midnight to return to my place in Ludhiana. There was hardly any visibility on the roads, as smog had completely enveloped the night.

I couldn't help but wonder: Can pollution be tackled without addressing the pollution of selfishness and personal interests that has consumed human minds?

I remain hugely optimistic. Nature has its own ways of handling things. It's not just about humans; it's about nature and Mother Earth, who knows how to balance things out. This has always been the case. For eons, the Earth has survived and will continue to do so. Humans are just one of the millions of life forms that inhabit this planet and may eventually perish with time.

However, I have a strong feeling that, having created humans as its finest creation, nature may want humans to survive longer. Therefore, it will eventually guide humans towards the right way of living. Does it matter if our generation exists to see or experience those beautiful times? Not really.

UNTITLED #188

"I want to be a corporate leader, RS," he said.

"Well, then, do one thing - make a promise to yourself that you'll get up in the morning and go for a walk at 6:00 a.m." "How is that important?"

"OK, if not that, then promise yourself to start something you haven't done yet and need to," I insisted.

"RS, I don't understand," he almost pleaded.

"Well, the first step is to learn to keep promises. So start by keeping those you make to yourself."

"Oh."

"For me, that's one of the key traits of a corporate leader - keeping promises."

With that, I completed my shortest module on Leadership Training.

UNTITLED #189

As he drove on the GT road in Ludhiana, navigating heavy traffic to drop me back home on the other side of the city after my session, I observed the older man who was completely focused on driving, looking straight ahead. He spoke to me a few times without losing his focus, fully engaged in his job to ensure the desired outcome - helping us reach our destination safely.

I wondered - would it be safe if he started looking around everywhere? Of course not, as there would always be a possibility of a collision or an accident.

And that's when, like a flash, a lesson appeared in my mind. Isn't this the reason for most of the verbal and intellectual accidents that occur in the corporate world? Most conflicts happen when one starts focusing on how others are working when one starts giving suggestions on how others can improve, and when one loses focus on one's own job.

One must stay focused on one's job, without diverting attention, just like my older friend.

UNTITLED #190

"RS, you mentioned somewhere that you learn a lot from nature. Can you share one such lesson?" He asked.

"Well, many have said it in different ways. However, I observed this and learned something a while back. I was standing on the edge of a tree's shade. It was hot. After a few moments, I found my face exposed to the sun. Oh, where had the shade gone? It had quietly moved to make space for the sun. Yes, there are moments when the sun moves to give similar space to the shade. There is never a conflict. I learned it was all about giving space."

"Oh, but it's not easy, RS. Is it?"

"Giving space must come to us naturally. It has taken me aeons to understand it. I've started practising the magic of 'pause' to practice acceptance and giving space."

"I think next time in a similar situation, I'll also practice taking that magical pause. RS, can you teach me?"

I did, of course.

UNTITLED #191

One afternoon, I was searching for a parking space near the bank I had come to visit. As I slowly moved along the edge of the road, I reached an area with ample space, but it was difficult to park because a man had parked his car in such a way that no other four-wheeler could fit. He was occupying too much space and seemed to be listening to music while sitting in the driver's seat. I decided to ask for his help. I stopped beside him, rolled down my window, and said,

"Hi there, can I talk to you?" I wanted his attention.

He looked at me, paused, and said, "Tell me."

I asked, "Is there a specific reason you parked your car this way? Are you saving space for your friends?" "Oh, no, not at all. I didn't notice."

So I said, "Well, now that you've seen it, can you help me?" "Oh, yes."

He moved and parked appropriately. Suddenly, there was plenty of space. As soon as I parked, another car followed suit. This highlights a major concern: we often don't realise how even our smallest actions and choices can negatively impact others. I'm sure many people passed by, fearing potential insults. We need to learn conscious behaviour.

UNTITLED #192

A new Executive Assistant was transferred to Mr. X, who was heading the Materials department, from another department.

This took place sometime in 1987 when computers were yet to be introduced in the company.

Mr. X was planning to visit some key suppliers in Mumbai, and he asked the new young assistant to prepare the files and papers for him. He gave instructions to collect data from some of the managers in the department.

After about a couple of hours, Mr. X found a file on his table. He opened it and saw that on the inner cover, a paper was pasted with the phone number of the hotel where he was to stay, as well as the phone numbers and names of the suppliers he was scheduled to meet, along with the times and dates. On the right side, the file started with an index of the filed papers/documents. Proper 'flags' were placed to create supplier-wise segments. He reached the last inner cover, which had another page pasted with four columns: Date, Supplier, Material Details, and Outcome of the meeting. Mr. X called the young assistant in and asked, "Have you undergone a professional course?"

"No, Sir, I haven't."

"Then how could you manage this?"

"Simple, Sir. I just thought if I were you, what would make me comfortable."

UNTITLED #193

There are days when you don't find stories. I usually think about what I want to share for the day during my morning walks. Today, I felt empty. Somehow, nothing seemed like it could be turned into a story.

Nevertheless, as I walked, I found myself doing everything I could to find inspiration, such as: looking up at the scattered clouds in the sky, listening to the birds chirping and leaves rustling as trees swayed in the cool breeze, stopping to enjoy the magnificent sight of blooming flowers; feeling the morning sun on my face; letting my thoughts take flight to find the first line of a new poem; focusing on how my feet touched the ground to experience walking meditation; and saying a happy hello to little children on their way to catch the school bus.

Despite all this, the story still didn't come. Yet, I felt good and happy. I wondered what was happening and where the positive energy was coming from, despite the emptiness I felt. That's when I realised that everything I was doing was in the 'present.' There was no past and no future. Oh, how I loved that state!

Yes, I found my story. Thanks to the morning!

UNTITLED #194

"My HR told me they prefer to work with established Training Companies. Labels matter, RS. I'm sorry," his tone was apologetic.

"Yes, you're right. Labels matter," I agreed with him. He seemed satisfied, and the apologetic look disappeared.

"You know I admire you. For me, you're among the best. But this is how things work."

"Yes, I know this is how things work."

"Wish I could really make people understand.""Wish you could. Of course."

"You don't seem to be troubled.""Should I be?"

"I mean, you need to get much more work than you're getting."

"Let's understand. You promised. You're not able to keep it. That's fine. It happens. We make promises out of emotions, and then we get stuck in details. I understand. So please don't feel guilty about it."

We need to be cautious while making work promises to someone like me if we're unsure about our own influence at work or elsewhere.

It's better to keep admiring, learning, sharing, occasionally conversing, being friendly, and mutually respectful. How beautiful would that be, right?

UNTITLED #195

"You're amazing, RS sir," he suddenly appeared before me and exclaimed.

"Oh, no, I'm not amazing. I'm amazed. How could I really grab your attention?" I expressed my surprise rather pleasantly.

His presence triggered a memory from a couple of years ago when, at a gathering of professionals, the same gentleman had royally ignored me and refused to even give me a chance to say hello. At that time, he was interacting with a more popular and highly successful executive. Perhaps, back then, I was a nobody to him.

"Don't say that, sir. It's an honour to meet you."

"Oh, I'm feeling so deeply humbled. Thanks a lot!" No, I didn't ignore him. I couldn't be the same person I had disliked at that time.

Well, things change. They do. Along with them, people's behaviour changes too. It happens, and it's okay.

So, don't be disappointed if you get ignored or neglected today. Keep doing your part. Doing - that is extremely important.

UNTITLED #196

"I want to know myself. I want to become self-aware. Can you help me?" he appeared quite serious about it.

Mr X listened and said, "It requires courage because the only concern about becoming fully self-aware is that one may not like whoever emerges from the darkness of ignorance. Do you have the courage?"

He just looked at Mr X, not speaking, as he seemed to be digesting the intensity of what he had been told.

Understanding his dilemma, Mr X continued, "That's why it takes courage to become self-aware; it's not a laughing matter. As you delve deep inside yourself, there are moments when it can be a little scary. But when your heart catches that first beam of light, there's nothing more beautiful.

That's when Pema Chödrön's words, 'You are the sky. Everything else – it's just the weather,' start making a lot of sense. And then you not only laugh but dance too. You experience the freedom of being YOU, drenched in myriad colours. You feel empowered to choose any colour you want, any time you want, because now you know who you are." Oh, he had already started feeling lighter.

UNTITLED #197

About a decade ago, I found myself resting on a hospital bed due to a hypertension attack. Mr. X, who was visiting me, smiled and said,

"OK. Done. RS, I saw it coming. It was just a matter of time. I never understood why you were always in such a hurry. It's simple – just slow down a bit. I'm sure you even think too fast. Always check yourself. Take a long breath and slow down. Slowing down a little means reduced stress, a quieter mind, and clearer steps forward. Don't rush; you won't miss anything." He took a pause and spoke those intensely golden words, "Trust me, RS, no one is really missing you out there, outside your home. No one ever waits. Those who need to, will. So, plan things in a way that you don't have to rush."

Then, Mr. X handed me a paper with this lovely quote by Lao Tzu: "Nature does not hurry; yet everything gets accomplished," and said, "Start by learning to walk slower. Your thoughts will become slower. For a change, let your body guide your mind. All the best!"

Such simple advice changed my life.

UNTITLED #198

The sky called out to me—vast and blue. I wanted to fly, and so I did. I didn't worry for a moment about my wings not being strong enough. The pull from above drew me into the unknown, and I loved it.

From then on, I would fly whenever I felt like it. No, I didn't soar high up there; I couldn't because my wings were still under construction. Yet, I was able to feel the wind on my face and let the sunbeams warm my heart. Whenever I grew tired, I would land on a soft, white cloud to rest for a few moments.

At times, I wanted to play, so I would slide down a rainbow. As the sun set, it would call me to descend with it and create melodies with the waves washing over the sandy shores. The moon, on the other hand, would invite me to climb up to it, holding a moonbeam that offered a passage to collect stars along the way. I chose the moon. In those moments of tranquillity, my heart, mind, and soul became one, and I revelled in the ecstasy.

Afterwards, I would return home to create my reality—a happier reality—every day. It's a joyful routine, these flights into the unknown.

UNTITLED #199

"How do you handle criticism of your writing?" "Criticism? What's that? Isn't it just another perspective?"

"Don't you get upset when some people make it personal?"

"No, I keep it impersonal. I believe my mood is my responsibility. People comment based on their own feelings or inner environment at that moment. They have their own justifiable reasons. I respect those reasons and respond appropriately."

"Does it help?"

"It keeps me at peace and helps me practice happiness."

And that's how a brief conversation about how I handle criticism came to an end.

UNTITLED #200

I refused to do what he wanted me to do, as it didn't align with my values. He became angry and, with glaring eyes, said, "RS, I haven't shown you my other face ever. Don't force me."

I replied, "Oh, you're a two-faced man, is it? Which one do you see in the mirror every morning?"

It seemed as if my words hung in the air for a moment before striking him hard, causing him to freeze like a statue.

After that, things unfolded as they should have. Sometimes, just a sentence or a word can change the way we act or perceive our lives—if only we're sensitive enough to recognise them.

UNTITLED #201

A couple of months ago, I unexpectedly encountered an acquaintance from the past while walking towards the luggage belt at Ahmedabad Airport. He had been following me on LinkedIn and suddenly asked, "Hey RS, why do you write every day on LinkedIn?"

I pondered his question, realising it was a 'why' question rather than a 'how' question. So I asked him, "How would my answer add any value to you or me?"

"Oh, no, I asked just like that."

This is something we need to work on—asking questions 'just like that.' Making this one change can significantly impact our lives.

Reflect on past experiences and interactions that left you feeling unhappy or dissatisfied. You'll likely find an unnecessary question at its root.

UNTITLED #202

"I made a big mistake."

"And you know it is a mistake"

"Yes, RS."

"Then it is no more a big mistake. Your awareness dilutes it."

UNTITLED #203

"RS, where have I ended up? No one listens to good ideas here."

"When did you join?""About a month ago."

"Were you given any advice on the do's and don'ts since it's the start of your career?"

"Yes, RS, it's true. A senior told me I should observe for at least six months before suggesting improvements."

"Did you listen to him?""No, but RS...hmmm..."

"Let me give you an example. It would be challenging for you and your family if a guest arrives and, while sipping tea, starts commenting on your living room's aesthetics and offers suggestions. None of you would appreciate it. It takes time to build trust. Why would it be different in a corporation where people aren't even sure if you'll continue for the first six months? Isn't it? So relax... and wait..."

He began to think and just smiled.

I hoped that he had listened to me. Ha, ha...

UNTITLED #204

"Sorry Sir, I wasted your time."

"Do you really think anyone can waste my time?" "I don't understand."

"You don't need to feel guilty. You requested to meet, and I chose to spend my time with you. Get out of this guilty mode."

Many of us continue to live in this guilt mode, particularly with our seniors. We keep apologising for the choices they make. Instead, let's stop doing that and maybe thank them for their attention rather than feeling sorry for having gotten their attention.

UNTITLED #205

I was talking on the phone with a dear friend from the LI community when he asked,

"How are things, RS?"

"Well, I'm happily struggling to live in a world I don't understand."

"OMG, what are you saying, RS?"

"Yes, in these times when the world of technocrats is focused on Artificial Intelligence, I find people spending energy on learning to be Intelligently Artificial. It's tough to deal with such people, my friend."

"Oh, dealing with Intelligently Artificial people! My God, RS, you've said something profound."

We spent time afterwards discussing the decreasing levels of authenticity in our conversations and behaviour as humans.

After he hung up, I wondered - Are there any other entities, besides humans, that can choose to be artificial? Can nature act artificially?

UNTITLED #206

It happened about three decades ago. I was discussing my self-appraisal with my mentor and felt a bit nervous as he reviewed the ratings I had given myself for various traits. Suddenly, he paused, looked at me, and said, "9/10 in Written Communication, Ramesh? Compared to whom?"

I replied, "Sir, this is in comparison to my peers in the company."

Naturally, I had been taught to think like that. Outperforming classmates in school was considered a significant achievement. "I would like you to compare yourself with the best in the organisation," he advised me.

I was taken aback and asked, "Sir, how would you rate yourself?"

He responded, "5/10."

That genuinely surprised me. "I consider you the best in the organisation, and you're giving yourself a five? Can I ask - compared to whom?"

He explained, "Compared to the top columnists who write in magazines and newspapers."

Feeling embarrassed, I said, "In that case, let it be 3/10 for me, sir." He smiled and remarked, "The only way to stay a learner is to compare yourself with the best, not just the best around you."

UNTITLED #207

The elevator reached the ground floor, and the door opened. As I stepped out to start my morning walk, my neighbour, a young businessman, entered the elevator.

I greeted him with a smile and asked, "How are you?" Without hesitation, he responded in a cheery voice, "I am awesome," as his face radiated morning freshness. I replied, "Wow, stay blessed."

As I continued walking for the next couple of minutes, I found myself still smiling and feeling energised. His positive vibes had rubbed off on me, making me feel so good. I realised the real power of feeling awesome, good, and happy. Without even being aware, you can sprinkle doses of positivity on others.

Know that you are awesome, and say it! You might make someone else feel the same.

UNTITLED #208

"RS, he was speaking ill of you behind your back."

"Why are you telling me?'

"Because you consider him your friend. You should beware of him."

"Him or you?

UNTITLED #209

"Are you happy?"

You're surprised. You pause. You think. Are you? Then you reflect. There were moments when you were happy, but not many. Yet, you always felt you were generally happy. However, doubt creeps into your mind. Is it true? Were you generally happy, or did you always end up arguing to prove to others why and how you were happier than them? And those arguments often took away the lighthearted feeling.

I learned to handle this question.

"Are you happy?"

"Yes, at this moment, I am." "What do you mean?"

"I mean that I am."

"What makes you happy at this moment?"

"Meeting you. Should I be unhappy meeting you? Why would you want that?"

UNTITLED #210

"If I cannot fly, let me sing." - Stephen Sondheim.

My interpretation of this beautiful quote:

Singing and becoming one with the song is as liberating as a flight into the vast skies, letting the winds take you wherever you desire.

For me, my mind is my sky, and I often enjoy such liberating moments.

May I reach a place where I can make each of my breaths sing life!

Oh, thank you, God, for these words that just happened, guided by the creative energy of all those who will receive and read them as I receive them from you now that you are reading them. I can feel your energy wherever I am in this moment of NOW.

Touch wood! God bless...

UNTITLED #211

I had a fascinating experience and gained some insight. Let me share:

I had just taken a cab to visit a friend in another city. As we drove through the day's traffic, the driver suddenly pointed out, "Look at that, sir, this Charitable Hospital was built by Mr. X and his family. Very generous, sir! My mother received treatment there without any financial burden on me."

We continued, and as we passed a large house, I noticed the nameplate and said to him, "Hey, this is Mr. X's house, isn't it? You didn't mention anything about it."

"He built this for himself, sir. How does it matter to anyone? Why would I talk about it?"

And then, a great insight struck me!

When you do something for others, people talk about it. When you do it for yourself, well, who cares?

UNTITLED #212

"RS sir, I want to reach the top."

"Then why stand here and waste time? Start climbing.." "I don't know how.."

"Ask someone who has been there."

"I am asking you.."

This is what happens. Half of our life, we spend asking and seeking advice from the wrong people by assuming things. And then time flies, and we regret it.

We can be kinder to ourselves.

UNTITLED #213

It began so well. January 1, 2018, the New Year, just after sunrise. The first thing I did as I left my home for a morning walk was to buy okra from a vegetable vendor, as requested by my spouse. I knew that by the time I completed my walk, the okra would be sold out. He was a popular vendor.

I did exactly what I always do. I carefully selected each piece to ensure that I didn't pick up even one bad piece. The vendor watched me intently and said,

"Sir, many people come and buy, but I've never seen anyone be so careful. You always take your time picking out vegetables." I listened and replied, "I do the same with my thoughts. I choose only those that make me comfortable. So, I must do it with everything I buy, including okra or carrots," as I turned my attention to the pile of fresh carrots.

"Thank you, sir. I'm happy to learn this lovely lesson on New Year's Day. I'll try to do the same with my thoughts."

"You're already doing it because I can see your thoughts in the quality of vegetables you bring, so fresh and clean," I said, genuinely appreciating his efforts. He felt so happy, and when I paid the exact amount, he gave me a Rs 5/- discount on his own. "Discount for you, sir," he said.

I don't think my New Year's Day could have started any better.

UNTITLED #214

What makes a person successful? There are countless books and articles detailing every behavior necessary to reach the top.

However, I'm more interested in discovering which behaviors change unconsciously once people become successful.

When they notice these changes, if they can, what do they do to return to their true selves?

Reaching the top of the ladder, if that's considered success; then what about those holding the ladder? God bless!

Have you ever been one of those holding the ladder or the one who reached the top? Is there something you'd like to share that may benefit others?

UNTITLED #215

My happy observations from my visit to South Goa.

Beautiful roads are beckoning one to keep going.

Branches of trees from both sides of the roads bless one to breathe fresh.

Tastefully painted colourful bungalows give one that magical feel.

A clean sea beach calling one out to run bare-foot letting grains of sand stuck on feet shine like tiny suns

A setting sun beckoning one to sink with it to come out of depths

Sweet, simple people proud of their culture and tradition, offering care and help.

Those wonderful taxi drivers are so keen to tell stories, leaving one spellbound.

Oh yes...

"Goa is more mesmerising for the tourists. We see the beauty every day," said a resident.

For me, it was an amazing experience. Someday yes, someday I will visit again. Yes, someone will invite you for a session. No, not a session on keeping one stress-free because I think that may not be a need there.

UNTITLED #216

While jogging, I came across a rose blooming gloriously, gently kissed by sunbeams. Wanting to appreciate its beauty, I naturally stopped and gazed at it intensely, practising what is known as deep looking. The poet within me stirred, and a haiku formed in my mind:

A lovely rose bloom

with the soft touch of a sunbeam;

happiness and joy

It was during those early morning hours that I realised I wouldn't have enjoyed this moment if I had continued running. I needed to stop and look. As the renowned Vietnamese Monk Thich Nhat Hahn said, deep looking cannot be practiced unless one stops running into the future and pauses to immerse themselves in the present moment.

I believe many of our daily problems and stresses could disappear if we learn to stop and look deeply into the present moment with a calm mind. In doing so, we experience true stillness. At that moment, I felt as though the rose was also practicing this calm, this stillness. As Eckhart Tolle famously said: Stillness speaks.

UNTITLED #217

There's an old tale about two ministers summoned by the King to attend a meeting with the emperor. As they walked towards the palace, one minister was happy, while the other was stressed. The stressed minister asked the other,

"Aren't you worried about what you'll say in front of the emperor?"

The happier one replied, "No, I'm not. I'll speak the truth." "But the King might have you killed."

"Who's to stop him?"

A young man, inspired by this story, decided to live by the same principle in the corporate world and ended up getting 'killed' by the 'king.' He continues to struggle in a world he doesn't understand. The story was written centuries ago, and perhaps the minister was single, without responsibilities or debts like a mortgage or car loan, allowing him to be brave. Our young friend didn't grasp this, became deeply inspired by the story, and paid the price for his bravery in the modern context.

We should read stories and learn from them, but we must be cautious when applying those lessons to our lives. We need to take full responsibility and have the courage to accept and face the consequences that may arise, especially in a world driven by pretenses and masks.

UNTITLED #218

"Why are you driving so fast?" I asked my friend. The office was just 2 km away.

"To save time," he replied.

"How much time will you save?" He thought for a moment and said,

"About 5 minutes." "And what will you do with that time?"

He glanced at me, didn't answer, and then quietly slowed down.

We often risk our lives and others by driving fast, sometimes just to compete with a stranger on the road. Moreover, while trying to save time, we don't even know how we'll use that saved time. Please, let's stop rushing.

As RS says:

It may take a bit longer. You will arrive stronger.

Think about it! Now, do me a favour. Practice reading this slowly once more. You read it quickly the first time, didn't you?

UNTITLED #219

The other day, my spouse and I went out for some evening snacks. We enjoyed delicious chaat and paani poori. Afterwards, my spouse asked for a water bottle, which I needed to get from inside the shop. I inquired about the price, and the man behind the counter said, "INR 20." I took the bottle, checked the expiry date out of habit, and noticed the printed price was INR 19. I smiled and handed him an INR 20.

He accepted it, and I asked, "What are you giving me for INR 1? Any good news or a good thought, a smile, or something else?" He seemed bewildered. Silently, he reopened the drawer and handed me a coin.

I'm sharing this small success story for the sheer pleasure it brought me and, hopefully, some smiles for you too. :)

UNTITLED #220

In 1975, I had just passed my board exam. I had spent a lot of time learning and playing table tennis (TT), and I was determined to get into the best college in Ludhiana that would offer me a chance to join the team. So, I went there alone, got the form, filled it out, and went on the day of admission. I got admitted without any elders accompanying me. I had declared my independence. I wanted to be a TT star and represent the country. I was focused and joined the state team in 1976.

However, in 1980, at the peak of my game, with opportunities opening up, things changed suddenly. The day I was declared the university team captain with finals yet to be played, I lost my mom. My dad, who was quite old, fell sick. I had to rush back home, leaving the tournament. After that, I had to deal with what life had in store for me, leaving my dream unfulfilled.

It's not always true that one can beat the circumstances to achieve one's goals, but one can learn to accept what life offers and live happily. I managed to do well in that regard.

Nevertheless, I continued to practice and even won a small local TT tournament at the age of 57.

UNTITLED #221

He noticed Mr X approaching from the opposite direction and remarked, "I have great respect for Mr X."

Curious, I asked, "Really? Any specific reasons?"

He responded, "It's his qualities. He's very careful with his words and always maintains a humble demeanour." Then, he greeted Mr X as he passed by us.

I inquired further, "So, are you trying to practice the same qualities?"

"Oh no, I'm not. It's difficult to be like him."

This made me wonder: Can you truly respect someone without trying to emulate the traits you admire in them? Or is it merely admiration? I'm posing this question to explore the idea further. Observing others' good deeds, listening to inspiring stories, or reading excellent books won't be helpful unless we put some of those lessons into practice.. To me, respect and learning are interconnected. Mutual respect implies mutual learning. What do you think?

Haven't we both learned something – me while writing and you while reading?

UNTITLED #222

As he approached from the opposite direction, I recognised him as an acquaintance. I offered a warm smile, but he just looked at me without returning the gesture. I playfully said, "Hey, I'm not asking for one of your smiles. Just give me mine back."

Feeling cornered by my relentless cheerfulness, he finally gave in and smiled genuinely from his heart. We both burst into laughter. At that moment, I realised that laughter is like a wave of smiles originating from deep within us.

UNTITLED #223

"You know, RS, there's always been this fear holding me back."

"Always? Since when?" I asked.

"Since I was a child."

I responded, "Back then, it must have been bigger than you. But now you've grown up. Has the fear grown up with you?"

He pondered for a moment, and then his eyes lit up as he exclaimed, "Oh my gosh, I never thought of it that way. No, I must be bigger than the fear now. Thank you for helping me realise this."

Indeed, change can happen in an instant. It truly can.

UNTITLED #224

"Sir, when you're not working, you must have so much free time. How do you get through the day without getting bored?" A young MBA student asked me.

I felt the need to provide an answer, so I told him:

"Let me share my routine. I wake up in the morning and pay my respects to the rising sun and the sky, then head out for a morning walk. I listen to the sounds of the morning, smell the fresh flowers as I pass by, greet people I encounter, and soak in some sun and fresh air before returning home. From my 11th-floor balcony, I say a cheerful hello to the city spread before me. Then, I enjoy a cup of tea with my spouse. I spend some time searching for news that catches my interest, and I usually find a few. That's how my day begins.

Throughout the day, I read, think, ponder, write, exchange thoughts, receive calls from across the country and even from abroad, update my presentations with new slides based on recent learnings, and respond to WhatsApp messages and emails. I also go to the market to pick up items and learn some lessons. My day is punctuated with delightful moments spent with my grandson. In the afternoons, I take a nap, and my evenings begin with my second and final cup of tea, followed by playing table tennis and other activities. I don't have a single moment of idleness, and I give 100% to every moment I live." He responded, "Hmm."

UNTITLED #225

There will come a time in life when you have the chance to share stories. When that time comes, will you recount borrowed tales, or will you have your own stories of joy, happiness, courage, love, and sacrifice? The answer is being determined today. May you live a life that allows you to create new, happy stories every day!

Let each of your stories have a happy ending. If you have one with a painful conclusion, you can revisit that memory and change the outcome to a happier one because, in the end, you learned something. If you didn't grasp the lesson at the time, you can do so now by reliving the experience in your mind and discovering what the lesson was. This will ease the pain and make you stronger.

Be a storyteller who shares more of your own stories. I emphasise share others' stories if you genuinely know their truth and as long as they don't come back to haunt you.

A NOTE OF GRATITUDE

I hope you enjoyed the stories and conversations. I'm sure you found yourself engaged in some of the discussions as well! Thank you for being a patient reader and thinker.

I am grateful to all the writers and thinkers from across the world and throughout history who have kept me thinking. I learn and continue to learn constantly. You have made me a learner and help me improve every day.

My deepest gratitude goes to nature, my greatest teacher. I learned two crucial lessons from her: First, the sun always rises, regardless of how dark the night is. Second, even my shadow changes sides and disappears when it's dark.

I owe my existence to my wife, Rosy. I hope she feels good about how after decades of happy struggle life is unfolding each day. My son Achint, daughter Tapsi and daughter-in-law Smiti, all contribute to my happiness by constantly giving me reasons to be joyful.

My heart soars at the mere thought of my grandson, Ivaan! Imagine the joy he brings me with his constant presence in my thoughts and in my life! Thank you, God, for this gift!

I feel blessed to have the support of many more angels who stood by me during difficult times – my friends and my wonderful extended family. They know who they are.

Thanks to Prudhvi Tej who volunteered to do proof-reading for this revised edition of the book.

Finally, I am able to make it available for my readers in India. I am thankful to the wonderful team at Notion Press for bringing my dream to reality.

In Gratitude!

Ramesh Sood,

Pune, Maharashtra, India

#simplySOOD™

www.ingramcontent.com/pod-product-compliance
Lightning Source LLC
LaVergne TN
LVHW041023150826
845672LV00001B/178

* 9 7 9 8 8 9 1 3 3 9 9 6 5 *